Divided by
PARTITION
United by
RESILIENCE

Mallika Ahluwalia is the CEO, curator and co-founder of the world's first Partition Museum, which opened at Town Hall, Amritsar in August 2017. The Museum has been listed in the 'Best of India: 18 Places to Visit in 2018' list by National Geographic Traveller India. She was recently awarded with an Excellence Award by Conde Nast Traveller and an ASEAN-India Youth Achiever Award for her work in honouring this history. Prior to this, Mallika worked in the field of health and education with some of the leading international development organizations, focussing on social policy that impacted the most marginalized households in India. She holds an MBA from Harvard Business School, an MPA/ID from Harvard Kennedy School and an A.B. cum laude from Princeton University in public policy. She lives in New Delhi. Three of her four grandparents were impacted by the Partition.

Divided by

PARTITION

United by

RESILIENCE

21 INSPIRATIONAL
STORIES FROM 1947

MALLIKA AHLUWALIA

RUPA

Published by
Rupa Publications India Pvt. Ltd 2018
7/16, Ansari Road, Daryaganj
New Delhi 110002

Sales centres:
Allahabad Bengaluru Chennai
Hyderabad Jaipur Kathmandu
Kolkata Mumbai

ISBN: 978-93-5304-142-7

Third impression 2019

10 9 8 7 6 5 4 3

The moral right of the author has been asserted.

Printed at Repro Knowledge Cast Limited, Mumbai

Contents

Foreword

There are many ways that the history of a nation can be told—either through the experiences of rulers, or the experiences of the ruled. For a long time, there was a belief, not just in our country, but abroad as well, that the history of a nation is that of the ruler—their victories and defeats and their attempts at nation building. No one was really recording the history of the people, and certainly not the history of the common people. It is only in recent years that we have found the immense value of trying to understand how people lived in different centuries—and sadly, while we can find the clothes and jewels of the emperors and nobility, we rarely find records of the lives of ordinary people.

Therefore, even in museums, we find enormous stone sculptures, grand paintings, and speeches and proclamations—but little evidence of how people were reacting to them. As we now know, there is often a vast difference between what is 'officially' out there and what actually happens. In this book, the CEO and curator of the award-winning Partition Museum, Mallika Ahluwalia, has compiled select stories from the thousands of Partition stories the Museum has recorded (and continues to record) to bring to us some truly inspirational stories. These stories are important because they speak of the triumph of the human spirit. In the world we live in today, with all its insecurities and upheavals, these stories are an important and inspirational reminder of how people have overcome their grief to emerge even stronger.

Sometimes people forget that this history of the Partition of India is not very old. All this happened just seventy years ago—and yet we did our best for many decades to airbrush it away. We, in fact, were doing great disservice to those who had gone through Partition as they were forced, by our silence, to also keep silent about what they had seen and what they been through.

They lost their homes, livelihood and friendships. Many saw extreme violence and death. Many died. Women and children were also not spared from the violence. Cholera and typhoid tore through refugee camps and shelters; a heavier than usual monsoon caused floods. There were not enough refugee camps, not enough hospitals or medical care. Millions suffered.

Yet, the stoic fortitude and idealism of the refugees was remarkable. Many Partition survivors still say quietly, 'Yes, we suffered, but at least we were alive.'

It is to the credit of the vast majority of the survivors that they did not display their frustration or bemoan the lives they had left behind. They retained their dignity, worked hard, stabilized their family situations, and got involved in nation building.

It is this quality of quiet dignity, and grace under enormous pressure and pain, that you will find in the stories in this wonderful book. These are people who have earned the respect of the country for what they have contributed to it; but we must also respect them for the fact that they made their journey to the top despite the terrible circumstances into which, through no fault of their own, they had been thrust.

Whether it be former Prime Minister Dr Manmohan

Singh, athlete Milkha Singh, former Deputy Prime Minister L.K. Advani, or so many others—they hid their traumatic experiences from the world and just carried on working—full of idealism and hope.

This book is particularly important for young people and we do hope they will all read it—to realize that one can lose everything, even at a very young age, and still reach for the stars.

These life-stories also offer us hope over adversity—and it is this message that embodies the spirit of this book as well as of the Partition Museum.

We do hope you will join us in applauding these wonderful men and women who lived through harrowing times, but did not lose their faith in their country or each other. We salute them all!

Kishwar Desai
Chair
The Arts and Cultural Heritage Trust
www.partitionmuseum.org
24 June 2018

Introduction

Stories of Resilience

Millions of people were impacted by the Partition of India. Each of them has a story. This book contains the stories of 21 extraordinary individuals who lived through the devastation of Partition, were deeply affected by it, but then went on to achieve greatness in Independent India. It features a prime minister, a deputy prime minister, a chief minister, a governor, a Grammy award winner, two world-record breaking sportspersons, three Padma award-winning artists and two businessmen who built multimillion-dollar enterprises, amongst other equally inspirational figures.

Each of these stories is unique. They differ in terms of the family backgrounds, their migration and rehabilitation experience at Partition, the opportunities they had access to and the career paths they chose. But the common thread that runs through them is *resilience*. These stories are a tribute to the resilience of the human spirit that bounces back even after facing great adversity.

History through People's Lives

The sad reality is that most often history in our textbooks and museums focusses on the history of nation states and leaders; the focus is on wars, and kings, and governments. But rarely do we find histories that look at *people*.

I have had the immense privilege of being part of a community movement in the last few years to create the world's first Partition Museum—and to create it as a *People's Museum*. What this means is that we use people's own voices, their artefacts, letters, photographs to tell history. The 1947 Partition of India was after all the largest mass migration in human history, which makes it a humanitarian tragedy of devastating proportions. It is, therefore, particularly important that the narrative on Partition includes people's voices and experiences.

The response to the Museum (which opened in August 2017 in Amritsar) has been overwhelming. It has received awards and has been featured on lists of top places to see in India, but the most heart-warming response of all has been that of our visitors, many of whom have joined forces with us to document and remember this *people's history*.

As the current CEO and curator of the Museum, I have had a ringside view as teams of volunteers have gone out over the last three years to record thousands of oral histories. When we started recording these stories, we knew of course that we would hear experiences of challenging migrations by train, kaafila (caravan) or bus, of difficult days at refugee camps, of the violence, particularly against women. But we also heard things that we weren't expecting. For example, I wasn't expecting to find just how many children and grandchildren had never heard the Partition experiences within their own families (the veil of silence runs deep). I was also not expecting to hear as many tales of humanity and kindness as we did.

And I was not expecting to feel inspired. In retrospect, of course I should have been. We know this generation lived through the worst of Partition, bore their burden silently and focussed instead on giving a better life to their children. Their stories are difficult, but also inspirational.

In this book, we have featured 21 such extraordinary individuals that we came across in our work on the Partition Museum. This book is a tribute to their grit and determination (and also to the countless others like them—both known and unknown). They were the real nation-builders who have put us today on the global map.

Who is Profiled in the Book?

Having decided to write a book on the subject, the difficult question was who to profile amongst the thousands of oral histories we had collected. Four criteria were chosen:

- The person should of course have been impacted by Partition.
- The person must have been highly successful in their chosen field of work.
- We should be able to record their story either first-hand or from a direct family member.
- As a whole, the collection of stories should represent a diversity of experiences.

On the first criteria, we have tried to include a wide set of Partition experiences to reflect the many ways that families were deeply impacted by Partition.

The heaviest burden was borne by those who lost their loved ones. Athlete Milkha Singh and former Prime Minister Dr Manmohan Singh tragically lost family members to the violence; Milkha Singh saw many of his family members killed before his eyes, while Dr Singh lost the most beloved grandfather who had raised him.

Many of those profiled in this book, though they were just children or young adults, saw stabbings or the immediate aftermath—corpses. Film-maker Govind Nihalani remembers the fleeting glimpse of a man falling with blood oozing out of his back; author Ajeet Cour, recalls the shock of hearing the shrieks of a man fatally attacked; artist Satish Gujral recounts the overpowering stench of decaying bodies; and lyricist-film-maker Gulzar cannot forget the half-burnt corpses that lined his neighbourhood streets in Old Delhi.

Almost all remember the fires that blazed through their hometowns in early 1947. Dharampal Gulati of MDH remembers standing on his rooftop seeing neighbours' shops disappear; Hero MotoCorp founder Brijmohan Lall Munjal lost his own shop in one such fire; and former Governor Ved Marwah recounts how they managed to douse an arson attempt on their home. All remember the slogans of *Allah hu Akbar* and *Har Har Mahadev* that rent the air, filling hearts with fear.

The migration journeys are also different. Five of the people profiled in this book were fortunate enough to be able to flee by plane; they were spared what the others witnessed on the ground. The most traumatic journeys were for those who came by train, bus or kaafila. Mountaineer Captain M.S. Kohli experienced the worst when their train was derailed and then fired upon, narrowly escaping death multiple times in the months that it took them to flee to India. Former Chief Minister of Delhi, Madan Lal Khurana remembers being saved by the Gurkha soldiers guarding their train. He also remembers the lack of water on the journey forcing them to drink from a dirty pond.

They lost their homes at Partition—the lives they had known, the friendships they had made. Artist Krishen Khanna cannot forget his youth in Lahore, and journalist Kuldip Nayar remembers a best friend left behind in Sialkot.

However, I have also chosen to include five stories of people who didn't migrate in 1947–48. For instance, Gulzar. He was already in Delhi in 1947, but he saw worst of the violence play out against his Muslim friends. His story is an important reminder that violence was being perpetrated, unfortunately, by all sides. Brijmohan Lall Munjal was living in Amritsar in 1947, but was doubly impacted by Partition because not only did he and his brothers lose their shop in the fires that blazed through Amritsar, but they lived in fear till their parents were able to safely make their way across the border by train from their home in Kamalia in the then newly-created Pakistan. The driving force behind Tata Consultancy Services (TCS), Faqir Chand Kohli was studying in Canada in 1947, and returned in 1951 to find his family's life completely shattered by Partition; he then focussed on re-establishing his family's economic stability. Author Manoranjan Byapari did migrate, but only in 1953. His story is important for many reasons that I detail below while discussing the fourth criterion—diversity. And there is former Minister from Uttar Pradesh, Hamida Habibullah, who brings in the perspective of a Muslim couple that chose not to migrate even though this meant separation from family.

The second criterion for the book was success in their chosen fields. Here, we defined success as really achieving the highest echelons of critical and/or popular acclaim in their area of work. Most of the people profiled in this book have received a Padma award, or an equivalent. While we chose many individuals that are household names, we also chose to include some who are not, but deserve to be.

The corollary of the above criterion, however, is that because we have chosen to profile individuals who achieved public success, we, by definition, have excluded all those families who were so deeply impacted by Partition that they could never recover from that devastation. Their exclusion from this book is by no means denying or diminishing the importance of their stories. By paying a tribute to those who could rebuild, we should not believe that those who could not were in any way less capable or less determined. It could be that their circumstances were so much more difficult, or that their Partition experiences so much more traumatic, or that they never got a mentor or an opportunity that could unlock their future. Those who started as poor, rural peasants, and continued to eke out a difficult living in a new land, or who struggled to recover from the mental trauma of losing their nearest loved ones also deserve to have their voices heard and acknowledged. I hope that readers who want to learn more about their stories will visit the Partition Museum, where we have put a particular focus on ensuring that the different sides and narratives to the Partition are included. This book, however, by design, has focussed on one of the narratives—it is about the story of Partition we do not hear that often—that of hope and rebuilding.

The third criterion for inclusion was that we must be able to record their stories by interviewing them or a direct family member. The reason for including this criterion was two-fold. First, very practically, most available sources do not detail their migration, refuge or rehabilitation experience as specifically as we wanted for these Partition profiles. Second, we felt that the stories would be much richer if we could include personal anecdotes and experiences. Thus, many extraordinary people we would have liked to have profiled could not be included. So many like Manoj Kumar and Rajendra Kumar have, unfortunately, passed away. But there are still many who we wanted to interview but couldn't reach in time for this book. They include Roshan, Prem Chopra and Krishna Sobti, amongst many others. The only exception we made was Lal Krishna Advani, whose 900-page autobiography provided sufficient detail and personal insight on his Partition and post-Partition experiences.

The final criterion was that, taken as a whole, the stories in this volume should represent a diversity of experiences. Specifically, there were four points of diversity I wanted to ensure.

First, that they took different paths in their lives. These individuals represent a wide variety of professions. Two authors, a poet, three artists, a film-maker, two career politicians, an economist-turned-politician, a social worker-cum-politician, a restaurateur, two corporate professionals, a lawyer, a journalist, two businessmen, a police officer, a record-breaking athlete and a mountaineer. How they achieved their success also varies.

The second variation was by geographic and socio-economic background. The book includes a range of different starting and ending points. The people in this book lived in 13 different cities/villages in 1947. After Partition, they moved to eight different cities.

Five people were born in villages or very small towns, and thus, bring a different perspective than those who grew up in the major cities of what is now Pakistan. Often in the macro-narrative of Partition, voices of marginalized sections are lost; author Manoranjan Byapari describes his experiences as a Dalit refugee.

We have one story of someone moving from Balochistan,

four from the North-West Frontier Province (now Khyber-Pakhtunkhwa), nine from (west) Punjab. We also included three Sindhi stories and a Bengali story. This was important because the Sindhi and Bengali experiences of Partition were very different from the Punjabi experience. While in Punjab, almost all the migration was concentrated in a very violent nine-month period between March and December 1947, in Sindh and Bengal the percentage of migration that happened in 1947 was much smaller.

Sindh in 1947 did not witness the kind of communal violence that raged through Punjab. While some affluent families did migrate and some chose to send women ahead to safety due to sporadic incidents of violence, the vast majority of Sindhis did not leave in 1947. However, by late 1947, with the arrival of a large number of Muslim refugees in Sindh, the situation started changing. These Muhajirs (refugees) living in crowded refugee camps began to forcibly occupy the homes of the Hindu Sindhis. A growing fear and two major incidents during December 1947–January 1948 became the trigger. Within the next few months, a million Sindhis fled to India. Over the next three years, a few lakh more families followed.

Lawyer Ram Jethmalani's story typifies the Sindhi experience to some degree. Like so many others, in 1947, he sent his wife and daughters ahead to Bombay to live with his in-laws till the situation improved. He himself chose to stay behind in Karachi and continue his work. But the riots of January 1948 in Karachi became the trigger for him to also leave.

Similarly, Bengal too had a very unique pattern of migration; unlike the concentrated migration in Punjab, Bengali migration occurred in waves spread over many years. While some refugees migrated in 1947, a larger wave occurred in the 1950s when the combined impact of communal riots, the language movement in Pakistan, everyday discrimination, and the tensions created with incoming refugees over land and other resources, caused millions to migrate. Dalits, who often did not have the resources to migrate, and could imagine no livelihood away from the meagre land they owned or tilled, had resisted migration till the early 1950s; they too now left in large numbers. Waves of migration also continued in the following decades, including around the Hazrat Bal riots of 1964, and particularly in 1971, and even beyond. Like so many other Bengali families, Manoranjan Byapari's family fled in 1953.

Ram Jethmalani and Manoranjan Byapari's stories also tell us about the particular challenges that Sindhis and Bengalis faced in rehabilitation. Ram Jethmalani talks about his work in voiding the Bombay Refugees Act, 1948 that restricted where Sindhis could live and work. Manoranjan Byapari talks about the infamous Dandakaranya experiment of the Government of Bengal, where refugees were rehabilitated in the dense forests of Chhattisgarh and neighbouring states. His tale of exploitation by adults around him, and the death of a sister due to hunger, are a heart-breaking reminder of the challenges faced by refugees in rebuilding their lives.

The third point of diversity was to ensure that women's voices and their experiences were captured. As a woman, I would have liked to see half of the stories in this book to be of women. However, it is an unfortunate truth of that generation that fewer women operated in the public sphere; the definition of success we have drawn for this volume, thus, excludes all those women who quietly played a pivotal role in rebuilding their families and providing the bedrock against which their husbands or children could achieve outward-facing success. However, we do see women's experiences reflected in two ways. First in Ajeet Cour, Anjolie Ela Menon and Hamida Habibullah's stories. Cour's battle against the dominating patriarchy all around her is inspirational at any place or time. Second, we also see glimpses of women's experience of Partition in different stories—Captain Kohli describes the palpable lack of women at the refugee camps since so many had been lost to honour killings; Satish Gujral describes both a mob's attack on a woman and his efforts in rescuing abducted women. In the Museum, we have dedicated a whole section to the particular experiences of women during Partition, including the violence against women, honour killing and abduction; we hope to continue to record more stories of pioneering women achievers also.

Finally, we wanted to ensure that we could also include the experience of Muslims who stayed back in India during the Partition. As riots engulfed many parts of north India, many Muslims had to take temporary refuge in a camp or a friend's home to avoid being attacked during the riots. Many became part of 'divided families', where half the family chose to be in India and the other half in Pakistan. Again, we have tried to tell these stories in two ways. First, through the extraordinary Hamida Habibullah's story. She recalls how during Partition violence, a Colonel in the army insisted on personally delivering milk and groceries to their house every day to reduce the risk of attacks, while another Sikh officer slept on the verandah at night to protect them. Second, through the other stories. Gulzar describes how his Muslim school friends were attacked in the riots that swept across Old Delhi; Anjolie Ela Menon talks about how the servants had to take refuge in the Purana Qila camp; Kuldeep Nayar recalls how he was almost lynched in Ludhiana when mistaken for a Muslim; and Krishen Khanna describes how one refugee was saved from a mob. A story that I would have loved to include in this book is that of Shah Rukh Khan's father, Taj Mohammad Khan. At a time when Muslim migration was mostly from India to Pakistan, he made the reverse journey. A staunch freedom fighter, he believed in the vision of a united India. This decision had economic consequences—he left behind his home in Peshawar and moved to Delhi—and the family struggled for a long time. While success didn't come in Taj Mohammad's lifetime, today Shah Rukh Khan is of course the Badshah of Bollywood, and one of the highest paid actors in the world.

Taken together, the lives of the 21 individuals profiled in this book paint a broad canvas of painful yet inspirational experiences.

What Can We Learn from These Stories?

These stories are inspirational in a timeless way. I hope, that for those not familiar with the human impact of Partition, these stories will give a visceral first-hand insight into the many ways that it devastated families. These stories include memories of the migration, refugee camps and the struggles in rebuilding. collectively build an understanding of what Partition meant to the millions it impacted.

But there are also enduring lessons on success in here.

One pattern that emerged for me was the importance of institutions and mentors. Govind Nihalani found a mentor in V.K. Murthy, Anjolie Ela Menon in M.F. Husain. Captain Kohli found his home in the navy that gave him the security to explore his love for mountaineering. L.K. Advani and Madan

Lal Khurana found their footing in the stability of the RSS structure, and F.C. Kohli in the Tata Group.

The second was that opportunity is 'sticky' (to use an Economics term)—that is, those who have had opportunities in the past, are able to get more opportunities in the future. This is, of course, not a surprising insight to anyone familiar with the literature on economic mobility as it has held true in every country at every moment in time, and so, was equally true at Partition. The stories do show that those whose parents were in government jobs, or were doctors, were more easily able to rebuild their lives, than those who came from less privileged backgrounds. Conversely, the stories also show that tragedy can devastate any household, and that oppression comes in many forms. Ajeet Cour married into an affluent household, but felt crushed by her husband's domineering misogyny and was devastated by the loss of a beloved daughter in a fire. Thus, both the starting point and the intervention of luck (or adversity) were important elements in the journey.

On the point of 'luck', it is an interesting thought experiment, for example, to imagine how the lives of these individuals would have been without the Partition, which can surely be described as a devastating intervention of adversity or 'bad luck'. Krishen Khanna most explicitly says in his interview that in a way Partition led him to the Progressive Artists' Group and painting. Is that true for others as well? Would Gulzar have gone to live with his brother in Bombay if Partition hadn't dampened their family's economic prospects? Would Captain Kohli have climbed the Everest if he was living in Haripur in the Frontier Provinces? We have no counterfactual statements of course. One viewpoint we have heard in many of the oral histories in the Museum's collection (not included here) has been that of women who used to live in the purdah before Partition, but came out of purdah afterwards out of sheer necessity and the economic imperative to contribute to the household. Adversity too, then, shapes lives and careers.

The third insight is of course just the unyielding drive needed for success. Captain Kohli's story reminds us that we have to persevere—he failed in climbing Mount Everest twice and faced near-death while trying, but still he returned for a third attempt. From Milkha Singh, I learnt the necessity of ceaseless practice. He reminds us that it's easy to look at success, without realizing the relentless endeavours that must underlie it. Dharampal Gulati speaks about the importance of keeping an unwavering focus on quality standards; this is what enabled him to transform a small store into a multimillion-dollar business. Brijmohan Lall Munjal taught me about the importance of dreaming big and then having the detailed drive to execute against that vision. And, Manoranjan Byapari's life-story exemplifies that it is never too late to change the arc of one's trajectory. Each of these stories carries a lesson on developing resilience and grit.

I hope you find each of these stories as moving and inspirational as I have.

Telegram: 'Father killed. Mother safe.'

Manmohan Singh

Born: 26 September 1932 at Gah, District Jhelum,
undivided Punjab (now Punjab, Pakistan)

*Dr Manmohan Singh was the Honourable Prime Minister of
India from 2004–2014.*

'My name is Manmohan Singh. I was born in village Gah, Tehsil Chakwal, District Jhelum, West Punjab. According to my school certificate, I was born on 26 September 1932, but there is some confusion about the date of birth because in those days there was no register and in some other place my date of birth is registered as 4 February 1932. However, there is no dispute about the year of birth which is 1932,' Dr Manmohan Singh, the former Prime Minister of India, states in his trademark down-to-earth manner.

Dr Singh was born in a simple agrarian family. 'My family were traditionally farmers, but since it was not very remunerative, many members of the family used to go to cities like Peshawar for whatever occupation they could get a hold of. My father also went to Peshawar and he became a clerk with a private firm.' Singh's father worked in a trading company that imported dry fruits from Afghanistan.

Tragedy struck Singh's life early. His mother passed away from typhoid when he was a young child. 'I have no recollection of her as I was too young, but after her death, I was taken to our village Gah where my grandmother and my grandfather brought me up and it is in their care that I passed my primary examination.' His grandparents doted on him, and he would accompany his grandmother almost everywhere.

Though they lived in a rustic earthen house of two rooms, Singh had a happy childhood here. However, since the village school only was till fourth class, Singh went to live with his uncle in Chakwal for fifth class, and then with his father in Peshawar from sixth class onwards. 'I was registered in Khalsa High School, Peshawar for my sixth class. I studied there till the tenth class, and I appeared in the matriculation examination for Punjab University from there.'

Singh remembers both Gah and Chakwal as peaceful mixed community areas. 'There were more Muslim families than Hindu and Sikh families in Gah, so there were two Mosques in the village, and one big gurdwara.' The economic disparity was visible though, as the Muslims were mostly tillers on the lands owned by Sikhs and Hindus.

As a teenager in Peshawar, Singh became increasingly attuned to world affairs. Punjab was a major source of soldiers for the Second World War, and the impact was visible in the region. 'There were several families who joined the armed forces, and whenever the solders came back they used to narrate stories of war and people used to gather around to listen.' However, Singh remembers discouraging his fellow students from celebrating the victory of the Second World War in protest against British imperialism.

In March 1947, when riots broke out in the Rawalpindi area, Singh's family was immediately impacted. His grandfather who had raised him was murdered in the communal riots that suddenly engulfed Punjab.

'All the Hindu and Sikh men were invited for a meeting with Muslims. But they used that opportunity to butcher all of them, so my grandfather died in the process. All male Hindus and Sikhs were butchered.

'My uncle who was working as a clerk in Chakwal with a private firm, he sent a telegram to my father. The telegram bore just four words describing how suddenly life had changed, "Father killed. Mother safe." I remember seeing that telegram, and that's how my parents got to know that something was happening in our villages in Gah, in Jhelum, in Rawalpindi District. March was the beginning of trouble in those areas.'

Telegram: 'Father killed. Mother safe.'

Singh's grandmother was saved by her neighbours. 'My grandmother took shelter with a neighbouring Muslim family. The next day my uncle from Chakwal got a police escort with him and went to Gah. He collected all the women in the village and dropped them to a refugee camp in Chakwal.' Not all the women in the family managed to escape. An aunt poured kerosene and burnt herself and her mother to avoid abduction.

Singh and his family left Peshawar in April to join his uncle and grandmother in Chakwal. He had taken his matriculation exam the previous month in Peshawar, despite the riots and violence, and was anxiously awaiting the results. Getting to the examination centre each day had been a harrowing experience, and Singh had hurried down the long road past corpses, aware of the risk of being attacked. However, because of the disturbances, there was now complete confusion as to when and whether the results would come out.

'At that time, there was talk of the Partition of the country, and therefore, after one or two months, my father decided to take our family to Uttar Pradesh to a town called Haldwani where he had some business contacts with some private firm who could help us find temporary rental accommodation.'

Around May–June, the family reached Uttar Pradesh by train. 'We passed through many important towns, like Lahore and Amritsar, then Saharanpur, then Bareilly, and finally to Haldwani.' For 14-year-old Singh, who had only seen three places—Gah, Chakwal and Peshawar—this was his first opportunity to see more of India. Because they had come a few months before Partition, the family managed to travel unscathed. 'We had no trouble on the train journey.' The family travelled light, 'Except some bedding that we carried in the train, we didn't bring many things with us. We didn't really think that we would be leaving Peshawar for good. We all thought sooner or later we'll all come back. That never happened.'

Once he had set up his family in Haldwani, Singh's father felt that he needed to go back to Peshawar to continue his business and look after his shop. The period from then till December 1947 was highly stressful for the young boy and his family. 'We had no idea where my father was. I used to go to the railway station every morning in the hope that he would turn up.' The riots and refugee crisis visibly escalated around them. 'We did not know where he was and what had happened to him.'

It was only by December 1947 that Singh's father made his way wearily across the border in a kaafila. Having left behind the business in Peshawar, his father needed to find a new source of earning. 'After my father came back from Peshawar, he was actively searching for opportunities to start a business. He chose Amritsar. He opened a kirana (grocery) store in one of the local markets.'

Singh, meanwhile, had still been hoping that somehow his results might be released. 'I was just 14 years old. I had taken my matriculation examination in the hope that events would settle and my results would be declared, but I was not in luck. Partition came in the way and Punjab University itself was divided into two parts. The new East Punjab University arranged for examination for matriculation in February 1948.' Singh had to make his way to Delhi to take the exam again.

In the meantime, he enrolled himself for his intermediate (equivalent of Class 11th and 12th) in Khalsa College in Amritsar. 'I took the medical option, but I didn't like the subjects, so after a few months, I left. I went and worked with my father in the kirana store, but I did not enjoy that either.'

Telegram: 'Father killed. Mother safe.'

By September 1948, when admission for the new batches started, Singh's matriculation results from Delhi were finally declared. He had performed exceedingly well and so managed to get admission in Hindu College, Amritsar. After receiving his intermediate and BA from there, he went to Punjab University in Hoshiarpur for his MA.

'I spent four years in Amritsar. There was a public library in the Town Hall*, and I would go there quite often to study. There were also a lot of intellectual activities and important meetings there.'

His family lifestyle was still very simple. Around them the city itself had been devastated. 'There were a lot of refugees in Amritsar. Many parts of the city were burnt down, one could see the burnt down houses. Other parts of the city were simply vacated by Muslims and so there were so many empty houses.'

By now, they lived in Majith Mandi, where his father had his shop, moving later to Kanak Mandi. Though many empty houses in Amritsar were allotted to refugees, the family had to make its own ends meet as they were not successful in getting any rehabilitation under the property claims process. 'We did file a claim but we did not get any property.' He did, however, get support from the government on his education fees. 'Hindu College gave me a concession that as a refugee I would pay half the fee.'

Ultimately, it was his deep interest in education, his perseverance, and his intellectual abilities that pulled him through. He stood first in the university in his MA in Economics. 'After this result, I was appointed as a research

---

*The Partition Museum is now housed in the Town Hall, Amritsar. The library also still exists.

scholar in Punjab University. I think in those days scholarships were worth about ₹176 per month and I was hoping to do research. But one of my teachers was very impressed with my performance in my MA examination and he said that I should be ambitious enough to aim for Cambridge for higher studies and that's how after one year I sought admission to the economics course in Cambridge. I was admitted in Saint John's College there.

'In September 1955, I travelled by ship for the first time. I went to England to complete the course in two years. I was the only student to obtain First Class that year. I did not stay in England because I had a contract with Punjab University. The university had allowed me to carry my research scholarship to England on the condition that on graduation, I would return to teach. If I didn't serve as a teacher, I would have to repay with interest all the money they had invested in me. So I came back and joined the university.'

But fate had other plans for Singh. In 1960, he returned to Oxford for his PhD in Economics. Then after a few years of teaching in India, he joined the UN.

Singh's talents as an Economist soon got him much attention. At the young age of 40, in 1972, he became the Chief Economic Adviser in the Ministry of Finance, and a few years later in 1976, he was appointed Secretary in the Ministry of Finance. By 1982, he was appointed Governor of the Reserve Bank of India, and after that, went on to head the Planning Commission from 1985 to 1987.

To everyone's surprise, the quiet economist, was appointed as Finance Minister by the then Prime Minister, P.V. Narasimha Rao, in 1991. In a previous interview to Mark Tully, Singh said, 'On the day (Rao) was formulating his Cabinet, he sent

Telegram: 'Father killed. Mother safe.'

his Principal Secretary to me saying, "The PM would like you to become the Minister of Finance". I didn't take it seriously. He eventually tracked me down the next morning, rather angry, and demanded that I get dressed up and come to Rashtrapati Bhavan for the swearing in. So that's how I started in politics.'

In his time as Finance Minister, Singh would become one of the main architects of India's modern economy. In 1991, India was facing a macroeconomic crisis. Singh and Rao worked together to liberalize the economy, remove the License Raj, and open it up for the modern capital markets.

Singh got a seat in the Upper House of Parliament in 1991 with this entry into politics, and has held this now for five consecutive terms. He served as the Leader of the Opposition in the Upper House from 1998–2004. In 2004, Singh was appointed by his party as the Prime Minister of India and completed two full consecutive terms—the only Prime Minister since Nehru to have done so.

For a boy from a small village in undivided India, Singh rose to the greatest heights both within the country and internationally. Repeatedly highlighted on lists of the 100 Most Influential People in the World, Singh found his feet through a quiet dedication and perseverance towards excellence.

While with the government and international organizations, Singh visited Pakistan a number of times. 'At Cambridge, I had many friends from Pakistan. One of them was Dr Mahbub ul Haq, who later became a very distinguished economist and Finance Minister of Pakistan. I was very close to him and in 1968, he invited me to visit him in Rawalpindi. I was at that time working for the United Nations in New York. This was soon after the war of 1965, so relations were still not very normal. I went back to some of the places in Rawalpindi which I had seen as a child, and one particular bookshop I had wanted to revisit. There was such goodwill at that time that the shopkeeper refused to take any money from me for the books.' Singh also returned to the site where his naming ceremony had taken place, the Panja Sahib gurdwara in the town of Hasan Abdal near Rawalpindi. 'I used to go there often as a child for Baisakhi and other celebrations—that's the only place I wanted to relive my memories of childhood.'

Singh has never gone back to visit his village of Gah. 'I did not go there because of the memory of my grandfather and the others who were killed for no reason. All the houses were burnt anyway, so there was nothing to go back for.

'My grandmother used to tell me that my mother, when she was still alive, was very good at making Phulkaris. My grandmother said that she had made a whole boxful of Phulkaris to be given at the time of my marriage. That was also lost in 1947...'

But home can never leave us completely. In his bedroom, in Delhi, hangs a watercolour of Gah given to him by the former President of Pakistan, Pervez Musharraf.*

*This fact is taken from the biography *Strictly Personal: Manmohan & Gursharan* by Daman Singh, Harper Collins, 2014.

Telegram: 'Father killed. Mother safe.'

We Had No Land, the Whole of Divided India Became Our Land

Lal Krishna Advani*

Born: 8 November 1927 in Karachi, Sindh (now in Pakistan)

Lal Krishna Advani was the Deputy Prime Minister of India from 2002 to 2004, and the Minister of Home Affairs from 1998 to 2004. He has been a Member of Parliament for four terms from the Rajya Sabha and seven terms from the Lok Sabha.

---

*As we were unable to interview Lal Krishna Advani, the sections in quotes are taken verbatim from his autobiography, *My Country, My Life*, Rupa Publications, 2003.

'I did not even celebrate India's freedom on 15 August, even though for the past five years, ever since I became a *swayamsevak* of the Rashtriya Swayamsevak Sangh (RSS), I had been dreaming of nothing else but the arrival of this day,' mourns Lal Krishna Advani in his autobiography. The uncertainty of Partition was looming large in Sindh, where Advani had been born and raised, as the province was to go entirely to Pakistan.

Advani was born in Karachi, Sindh on 8 November 1927 to Kishinchand and Gyanidevi. Kishinchand had four brothers and all were well-settled. While he and one of his brothers were businessmen, another was a lawyer, one a professor of Chemistry in a major college in Karachi, and one a civil servant. Advani recalls that their house—named 'Lal Cottage' as it had been completed soon after Advani's birth—'was a fairly spacious, beautifully-designed, single-storey bungalow...[with] a horse-driven Victoria at home.'

Tragedy struck the young boy early with his mother passing away when he was only 13. However, living in a joint family system, Advani did not feel a paucity of love. 'The most vivid memory of my early childhood is the affection I received from everyone in the family, including my grandparents and [aunts].'

Advani studied at St Patrick's High School for Boys, which was the highest rated school in the city, from 1936–42. He excelled in his studies and completed his matriculation at the age of 14.

The memories of this school stayed with Advani for a long time. Decades later, he revisited it. 'I was able to visit my school during my brief trip to Karachi in 1978 as India's Information and Broadcasting Minister. All those teachers who had taught me attended a special reception... It was after a gap of 36 years that I was stepping onto the premises of my school, every nook and corner of which was so fondly familiar to me.'

A few decades later, and over 60 years after he matriculated, General Pervez Musharraf, also an alumnus of the same school, gifted Advani a memento of his school days. 'It was an album of documents and photographs from my school years, and contained, besides my school admission certificate of 1936, photographs of my teachers and principals.'

But in 1942, all these events were far in the future. The 14-year-old Advani enrolled in the Dayaram Gidumal National College in Hyderabad after matriculation. Because the Quit India Movement was underway, the college was often closed, and Advani spent a lot of time in the college library. 'It is here that my lifelong love for books began,' he remembers.

It was also here in Hyderabad, in 1942, that Advani joined the RSS. Though he had gone merely out of curiosity with a friend for the first meeting, Advani was drawn in by what he saw as the idealism and nationalism of the organization. 'One day, as I, along with the other volunteers, sat listening to the bauddhik (intellectual) talk by one Shyam Das, he posed us a question: "You receive so much from society, but what are you giving back? Isn't it your duty to do so? India is now under foreign rule. Isn't it our responsibility to liberate our Motherland?" His words gently opened a new door with my inner self and set me on a path of self-enquiry.' Advani remembers this as a defining moment in his journey.

He threw himself wholeheartedly into the organization's work. Within two years, he had become a full-time pracharak (organizer) in Karachi. By January 1947, he was the City Secretary; this involved monitoring the rapidly growing shakhas (daily assemblies) across the city.

Advani led teams of volunteers to discourage people from leaving their homes and migrating east. But by September, as streams of refugees started arriving in Karachi, the fear of attack grew stronger by the day amongst the Hindu population. The tales of violence, massacres and misery from Punjab unnerved the population; affluent families started sending family members ahead to safety.

Advani himself fled Karachi on 12 September 1947. He was barely 20 years old at that time. He could have not known at that time that it would be decades before he could return. His family was still in Karachi. The reason for his hurried departure was a bomb blast that had taken place a few days before in Karachi. Twenty people from the RSS had already been arrested. 'I had known nothing about the blasts. Nevertheless, since the local press started to level wild charges against the RSS, my colleagues advised me to leave Karachi. Accordingly, I left for Delhi by air on 12 September... This was my first ever journey by plane, made more memorable by the fact that I was travelling as a refugee from Pakistan, like millions of others, seeking shelter and a new beginning in a truncated India.'

Advani's family also migrated soon after. They settled in Mandla in Kutch, where his father was allotted some land through the Sindhi Resettlement Corporation. Mahatma Gandhi had convinced the Maharaja of Kutch to donate some land for the Sindhi refugees. Advani's father, Kishinchand, also worked in this Corporation.

But when Advani got on that plane in mid-September 1947, he did not know this. All he knew was that he was leaving his family behind, and also his childhood experiences of Clifton Beach and Manora Island, as well as an idea of Sindh that was based on an 'ethos of religious harmony, pluralism, mutual tolerance and peaceful coexistence'. The Sindh he had grown up in was one where Jhule Lal Krishna (a Hindu spiritual leader) and Shahbaz Qalandar (a Sufi saint) were equally worshiped by both communities. 'Religious fanaticism was foreign to both Muslims and Hindus in Sindh'. (Later, after he was married, Advani found that his own mother-in-law was also a devoted follower of a Sufi saint, Sain Qutab Shah. She sang Sufi kalaam with equal piety as Hindu hymns. Advani's sister-in-law and her husband also visited Pakistan regularly to pay obeisance at the dargah of another saint, Sain Nasir Faqir.)

On the afternoon of 12 September 1947, Advani and an RSS colleague landed in Delhi, a completely unfamiliar city, around noon. The extremely organized nature of the RSS structure helped them. Though they didn't know where the RSS offices were, they had the names of the two most senior leaders in the RSS in Delhi. They found their way to the nearby Delhi cantonment, and started asking around for any RSS workers. They found one who took them to his home, fed them and then took them to the local leader.

Advani was soon sent to look after the Sangh's activities in Alwar city in Rajasthan; this later expanded to include the entire district, and also a neighbouring district. '[This work] necessitated constant travelling. Many places were accessible by bus... However, there were other places to where the only mode of transport was either a bicycle or a camel.' Advani has many memorable experiences in all the small towns he found himself. Sometimes bathing with snakes in a pond, other times sleeping in an open goods train to reach his next destination. 'I learnt to live frugally,' he says.

The RSS thus became Advani's safety net post-Partition,

ensuring that he found his feet, a community and a way to support himself in his new life and city. But his political work would, by equal measure, throw thorns in his path. The first came in early 1948 itself.

Days after the assassination of Mahatma Gandhi, RSS pracharaks across the country were arrested. 'I was incarcerated in Alwar Central Jail... I spent the next three months there in the company of ordinary criminals...Prison life was hard. The greatest source of our discomfort was the food, which consisted of only three thick rotis and tasteless dal, served twice a day.

'After my release in August 1948, I spent the next four to five months underground...Underground existence was one of the most harrowing experiences of my life. The biggest trial was finding a safe roof over our heads. Within a few days of staying in anyone's house we would hear the same story: "Sorry, we cannot let you stay here any longer..." Householders were understandably afraid of imminent raids by the police... I soon lost count of the number of houses we changed while moving incognito in Alwar and Bharatpur.' Advani and his colleagues came out of hiding only the following year when the ban on the RSS was lifted.

In 1952, the year after the Bharatiya Jana Sangh was formed, under the encouragement of his political mentor, Pandit Deendayal Upadhyay, Advani became a political worker for the newly formed party. This was the first step in what was to become a long political career ahead. He worked on the first general elections in 1952, and has participated in every general election the country has held since then till date. In 1957, he moved to Delhi to support the party's MPs with their parliamentary work; soon he became General Secretary of the Delhi unit.

In 1960, worried about his financial ability to support his father who was nearing retirement, Advani spoke with the party leadership about his concerns, and switched over to the party magazine *Organizer* as Assistant Editor. Under an existing government scheme for journalists, Advani was able to get a flat, and could thus start to save from his salary of ₹350 per month.

On 25 February 1965, he got married to Kamla Jagtiani. 'In the aftermath of Partition, her family had to flee in extremely trying circumstances, reaching India in a dispossessed condition. Kamla's father, Premchand Jagtiani, a noble soul who did not take any compensation from the government for his lost property, passed away in 1952. Thereafter, she took upon herself the task of looking after her family. She worked in the General Post Office, first at *Gol Daak Khana* in Delhi for eight years and, later, near V.T. station in Bombay for nine years. Thus, like me, Kamla too, was used to living a hard life.' Within two years, they had two children.

In 1966, the first ever elections were held to the Delhi Municipal Council. Advani played a key role in the party's campaign. In recognition of this work, the party nominated him as Chairman of the Delhi Municipal Council, his first political office. In 1970, he was nominated by the Jana Sangh to the Rajya Sabha.

In 1973, some 30 years after he joined the RSS, Advani became the national President of the Bharatiya Jana Sangh. He would continue to rise in the national political landscape. He became India's Information and Broadcasting Minister in 1977, the Home Minister in 1998 and Deputy Prime Minister in 2002.

This success did not come easy or overnight. It involved many trials, like being jailed for 19 months during the Emergency.

It also involved decades of hard work and dedicated political activism. Advani was merely 14 when he started volunteering for the RSS, he was around 75 when he became the Deputy Prime Minister—a six-decade-long journey. It is a testament to his dedication that a young refugee boy from Sindh worked his way up through the party ranks to scale these heights.

Advani fully embraced his new home. 'Partition was a double-tragedy for the Sindhi Hindus... We had no land of our own, or, rather, the whole of divided India became our land,' he wrote in his autobiography.

Courtesy: Wikimedia Commons/Jorge Royan

I Owe My Life to an Unknown Gurkha Jawan

Madan Lal Khurana

Born: 15 October 1936 in Lyallpur, undivided Punjab
(now in Pakistan)

Madan Lal Khurana was Chief Minister of Delhi from 1993 to 1996. He has also served as Governor of Rajasthan in 2004. In 1961, he and Raj Khurana were married in Delhi. As Madan Lal Khurana is unwell, his wife, Raj Khurana, narrates his life story.*

---

*We have also drawn on a personal account of his Partition experience written by Madan Lal Khurana himself in 1997

'I owe my life to an unknown Gurkha jawan but for whose bravery and presence of mind I would have never escaped the clutches of death. Whenever I think of that train journey, when there was human carnage all around me during the Partition riots, I cannot but thank this young soldier who jumped in and saved a lot of lives.' Thus starts an article written by Madan Lal Khurana published on 14 December 1997 in *The Hindustan Times*.

Madan Lal Khurana was born in Lyallpur (now in Pakistan) on 15 October 1936, to S.D. Khurana and Laxmi Devi. Raj Khurana was born some seven years later, on 24 August 1943, in the nearby town of Sargodha (also now in Pakistan). They would only meet decades later on the other side of the recently drawn border, when they got married in Delhi in 1961. Their life together these last 57 years has seen many highs and lows—from the heights of serving as a Chief Minister and then a Governor, to the lows of being jailed during the Emergency and to his current ill health.

But back in 1947, none of these highs or lows could have been predicted. Then, the Khurana family was living in Lyallpur. S.D. Khurana had built a comfortable-enough life for his family on the income he earned from his soap factory there. But that comfortable life would soon be disrupted by the Partition, and they would have to leave their home for good.

By early 1947, when riots started breaking out across Punjab, and the situation was already starting to look grim, S.D. Khurana decided to send his two daughters ahead to safety. 'As soon as the rioting and the violence started, and the situation started to get worse, he sent his daughters to his brother's place in Amritsar,' says Raj Khurana. Madan Lal was

11 years old at that time. 'As Khuranaji [Madan Lal] was still studying at that time, he stayed back with his parents.'

S.D. Khurana, like many others, believed that they would be able to stay on in Lyallpur even after Pakistan got Independence. The family was, therefore, in Pakistan on the day of its Independence. Madan Lal writes in his article in *The Hindustan Times*:

'Freedom came but it didn't bring anything for us. When the entire nation was rejoicing in this new-found freedom, for us there was death all around us. It was no time for us to feel happy when so many of our people were killed... I saw the naked dance of death, the arson and mindless looting happening right in front of me. Hindus and Muslims were thirsty for each others' blood. On the one side there were young Hindu boys, armed with swords and pistols, and on the other side there were the Muslim youngsters, both sides busy inciting people with their slogans and speeches, beseeching their people to kill everybody on the other side. I remember the days when we used to keep a midnight vigil so that our locality was not attacked, so that we do not lose anybody from our locality,' wrote Madan Lal in his article.

Their family too was forced in September to take refuge in a camp set up in a nearby school. They left only with a few items for their daily use. 'It never occurred to us that we were leaving our homes for ever,' recalled Madan Lal in his 1997 article.

One evening, an attack at the refugee camp left many dead. The Khurana family realized then that they could no longer stay in Lyallpur. They boarded a special refugee train from Lyallpur to Amritsar. The train journey, though, was fraught with anxiety. The train would stop frequently, leaving it vulnerable to attack. 'That day, the train had stopped in the middle of a jungle, there was no station. I was young and in the middle of the night I felt very thirsty, I still remember how all of us were forced to drink the dirty water from a rain clogged pond.

'There were about half a dozen Gurkha jawans in our train. When it reached Lahore, there was an attack on us. For about half an hour there was an exchange of fire from both sides and all through this, we were simply remembering our gods. There was nothing much we could do and there was also this realization that the jawans on our train couldn't have held on for a long time. It was at this point of time that one of these jawans jumped out of the train, ran up to the drivers' cabin, put his revolver on the driver's forehead and threatened him to start the train immediately. There were more mobs on the way to Amritsar and therefore, they decided to divert the train to Ferozepur via Kasur. We were thus saved but I am never able to forget that half an hour in our life when we were literally hanging between life and death. If it was not for that young soldier, none of us would have survived that ghastly attack,' recalled Madan Lal Khurana in his article 20 years ago.

Raj Khurana adds, 'They somehow managed to make their way from Lyallpur to Delhi by train. They got down at the Old Delhi railway station, and started looking for an abandoned house that they could stay in. But every house they entered they found dead bodies. My father-in-law was a very religious man who believed strongly in the Hindu tenets of purity, he decided that the family could not stay there.' Refugee camps had sprung up around the city, and thousands of miserable, terrified refugees were streaming in every day. 'The schools were emptied to become refugee camps, but the signs of death everywhere were unbearable for my father-in-law; he decided he didn't want to stay there either.

'Somehow they made their way to Allahabad.' Her father-in-law had been there before to buy raw materials for his soap business, and so was somewhat familiar with the city. Once there, the family found an evacuee house and moved in. The family restarted their soap business here as well. 'Khuranaji restarted his education. After matriculation, he did both his BA in Economics and MA from Allahabad itself.'

Madan Lal's parents often reminisced to Raj about the life left behind. 'They would talk about the factory they had lost. They had to start from scratch here. They had no money, so it was difficult,' she says.

Madan Lal had already joined the RSS in Lyallpur. Now, in his new surroundings, he joined its local shakha, and also started getting more involved in politics. 'He stood in the elections for the student council at Allahabad University and won. Through this he got to meet some of the important leaders of that time, like Jawaharlal Nehru, so his interest in politics also kept increasing over time.' In 1961, at the age of 25, Madan Lal married 18-year-old Raj Khurana in Paharganj, Delhi. By this time, the family had moved to Delhi, and he was actively involved in politics.

'We used to live in Paharganj initially, near the railway station. We had taken up a small house. He was involved in politics completely by the time we got married. He would return home at midnight or later every day due to his work. For a long time, I found it very strange since no one in my family had ever been involved in politics.' A young bride of 18, Raj was challenged by her new reality. 'His work included a lot of field work, and on-ground campaigning. Unlike politics today where people join a party and ask for a ticket after two or three years of work, he started as a zameeni karyakarta (field worker). "I will only take on the responsibility when I am fully prepared for it", he used to tell me.'

Meanwhile, Madan Lal also needed to sustain his family. 'He got some good job offers but he did not want to take them up because he felt he would have less time for his political work. He took up the job of a teacher at a government-aided school.'

The dedication to the party did not go unnoticed. In 1965, Madan Lal got a formal post in the Jana Sangh party, becoming the General Secretary of its Delhi chapter. This was followed soon by running for election in Delhi. He became a member of the newly formed Delhi Metropolitan Council in 1966. He retained the post till 1989, when he became a Member of Parliament. It was this political career, which had started from his student days in Allahabad, that led Madan Lal to re-establish his feet firmly in Delhi as a post-Partition refugee.

Though without family wealth to fall back upon during these days of activism, both Madan Lal and Raj Khurana had to be content with a very simple lifestyle. Raj also had to learn to fend for herself, while Madan Lal toiled day-in and day-out for the party.

Lightning does sometimes strike the same spot twice. In 1975, Madan Lal would see exile for a second time. When Emergency was declared in 1975, there was a crackdown on political activity. A warrant was issued for Madan Lal's arrest. 'It was a difficult time because he stayed underground for six months. He was in hiding. He used to stay at one place and then another because he had warrants against him. But even in that time, he didn't fear anyone, he kept thinking about how to help others. He used to send out pamphlets informing people that if they needed help they could go to such and such a person for help. For six months he continued doing this, but eventually he got arrested.

'[They] demolished our house as well. We were living in Kirti Nagar. They took away everything, even the curtains. They took away our fridge, our TV, the children's toys. My children were only five or six years old at that time. They brought trucks and took away all our belongings. Even the things that were kept inside our fridge, like milk, etc., were thrown outside. They took it away because they believed that if they troubled us, Khuranaji would come back. I remember it was raining when they came. They told us to sit in the garden outside our house. Then they put up the forces all around the house so that no one could even come to help us. I asked them if we could go inside to get some bags, but they would not even let us enter. I sat outside with the children in the rain.

'Then our bank accounts were sealed. It was basically like we had nothing. He was in jail for about fourteen months. I remember going to Tihar jail to meet him. You had to get an appointment beforehand.'

For Raj, who was then only 32 years old, these experiences were a tough jolt. She had grown up as the only daughter in her family and had lived a fairly protected life. 'As I faced these situations I slowly learnt how to cope over the decades,' she says.

Looking back on her husband's career, Raj is content, despite the many tribulations it brought. She attributes his success to his strong value-system rooted in culture and traditions. 'It is a question of honour and dignity. He never had any greed. We used to live in a small house, but [he] would attend to everyone, so everyone used to love us. When someone gives you honour or respect or love, that is real life, that is what motivates you to work harder. A political life is hard to get used to in the beginning, but eventually, seeing the love, we started feeling better.'

Madan Lal did not return to his birthplace for some 60 years. 'He went to Lyallpur for the first time after Partition in 2006. He took me along with him and he showed me the location of his house and their shop and showed me around the town... But it had changed a lot. A lot of the older buildings had been demolished,' says Raj. But even though he had not returned, the people of his hometown still took pride in his achievements. Madan Lal wrote in 1997: 'I once appeared in Rajat Sharma's *Aap Ki Adalat* on Zee TV. In his introduction in the beginning of the show, Rajat mentioned that I was born in Lyallpur in 1936. You cannot imagine my happiness when Rajat told me a couple of days later that Zee TV had received hundreds of letters from Lyallpur congratulating me for attaining such a high position in India. They were all very proud of me.'

Defying Death, Scaling New Heights

Captain Manmohan Singh Kohli

Born: 11 December 1931 in Haripur, Hazara
in the North-West Frontier Province
(now in Khyber-Pakhtunkhwa, Pakistan)

Manmohan Singh Kohli set a number of world records in mountaineering, including leading an expedition that put nine people at the top of Mount Everest in 1965—a record that was held for 17 years. He received a Padma Bhushan and Arjuna Award for this feat.

In the North-West Frontier Province of undivided India (now the Khyber-Pakhktunkhwa province of Pakistan), amidst lush green pastures, with mountains all around, and the Indus flowing a few miles away, lay a small town called Haripur Hazara. In this scenic setting, Manmohan Singh Kohli was born on 11 December 1931.

Kohli's mother died when he was only three years old, so he was brought up by his father.

'My father performed the duties of both a father and a mother. He sacrificed his own life. He was only 39 when my mother died, but he never remarried because he did not want us to be mistreated by a stepmother.' Kohli's father had a deep influence on him and he imbibed his spirituality and his beliefs in a simple, active life.

The town was well-integrated and different religious communities lived peacefully most of the time, barring a few incidents. One such incident occurred in 1943 when the birth anniversary of a Sikh Guru coincided with Muharram. The joyous celebration of the Sikhs and the mournful procession of the Muslims passed each other peacefully in the morning, but in the second half of the day, miscreants descended on a local Gurdwara, killing a priest. They also burnt the Guru Granth Sahib. The situation could easily have flared out of control, but that was averted owing to swift action by the police.

But by 1946, things were going awry. By the start of 1947, killing of non-Muslims had become commonplace. The creation of Pakistan seemed imminent, and non-Muslim families slowly started migrating eastwards. By March 1947, 'with daily killings, we were wondering whether we too should immediately leave to save our lives.'

Defying Death, Scaling New Heights

The dilemma facing the family was that Kohli's matriculation exams were a mere few weeks away. 'We finally decided that my career and life would be very adversely affected if I did not appear for my matriculation examination. We had, in our family, complete faith and belief that a genuine ardas (prayer) never fails. And so my father went to the Gurdwara, did the ardas and we decided to leave only after the examination.'

But it was not easy to take the exams. A week before the exams, a minor altercation resulted in 50 deaths, so stepping out of the house became nearly impossible.

'I had to be very careful and go through the mohallas secretly to reach the examination hall in my school, which was almost a kilometre away from my house. When I got there, I saw almost half my classmates were missing; they had left Haripur and had gone [east] to save their lives.'

The atmosphere in the examination hall was charged. With the general breakdown of law and order outside, even inside the classroom, Kohli recalls, some students 'kept their pistol and dagger on the table and cheated openly'. Every day for a whole week, Kohli went through the same ordeal, unsure whether he would make it to school safely in the morning and make it to home safely in the evening.

Despite the trying circumstances, Kohli completed his exams. 'Immediately afterwards we left Haripur and came to India.* We spent a month in Patiala, a month in Haridwar and a few days in Delhi.'

---

*As this was pre-Partition, it is anachronistic to say they went 'to India' as Haripur was still at that time in undivided India; therefore, the sentence should be read to mean that they came eastwards.

The challenge remained that he couldn't get a job till his results came out. 'It was about the middle of July, nearly three months after we had left, and I had been going from pillar to post looking for a job, but everywhere they said, "Unless you have your matriculation exam result, we cannot employ you." So, finally, when we heard on All India Radio the leaders announce that they were going to control the riots, and people should go back to their homes, there was a big discussion in our family of three. My father and I were keen to go back to Haripur. My brother didn't want to risk his life again by going back.'

'My father and I were also in two minds. We went to the Gurdwara Sisganj in Chandni Chowk [in Delhi], and we prepared two folded papers there, one said "Return to Haripur", and the other, "Stay in Delhi". We asked the head priest to perform an ardas for us, and then to select a chit. He selected the first one.'

That was how father and son decided to return to Haripur. Kohli's brother decided to stay back.

During this time, Kohli would also fortuitously manage to obtain his matriculation results. One day, while waiting to switch trains, Kohli saw a bookstall at the station. 'There was a Gazette there and in bold letters, it said "Matriculation Results Inside". The problem was that I had no money. So I waited till the owner went to the toilet for a minute, and then I picked up the paper and quickly boarded the train. In five minutes, the train left. The first thing I saw was my result.' Kohli soon realized that all other students would also be anxious to know their results. 'I thought of a novel way of making money. I put up a big board when we were near Har ki Pauri, "Matric Results for Four Annas", and there was a one-mile-long queue...'

We used to have no money in those days, but that evening, after a long time I had a good feast.

'When 14 August came, we were back in Haripur. We happily participated in the Independence Day celebrations. I was looking forward to now becoming a Pakistani citizen.

'On Independence Day, about 50,000 people gathered in the parade ground. The local leaders of Muslim League came to give speeches: they said that now Allah had given us our own country, Pakistan, we should pray to Allah that he keeps this country very happy and prosperous. People were shouting slogans and so on. Everyone was dressed well, like it was Eid. They were celebrating, they were happy. And I was happy too. My father and I were content because now we could continue to live in our own town. My entire 16 years had been spent in Haripur, surrounded by its hills, so, naturally we were excited that we could continue to live at home.'

But less than two weeks later, the idyll was shattered.

'On the 26th of August, a Muslim family friend came running to our shop and told my father "Leave immediately! A big mob of a lakh people is coming and you'll be killed on the spot." Since the Gurdwara was opposite our shop, we ran towards it, and just about managed to get in and close the door from inside when these men came running and nearly caught us.'

That night, recalls Kohli, thousands were burnt alive in the town. 'All of Haripur was set on fire. All the shops and houses were burning.' The sky turned orange with the flames.

By evening, the fire had reached the Gurdwara also. 'We realized we needed to reach the police station. So at night, we jumped from one terrace to the other, and made our way very gingerly towards the police station. It took us the whole night since we had to avoid being seen.

'But finally, at around six in the morning, when we jumped out on the street 50 metres from the station, a mob saw us and charged at us. We somehow managed to outrun them and reached the police station.

'We were kept there the first day. On the second day, we were taken to the town fort. There were maybe some 20 to 40 other families there. A few days later, a truck came, and we were taken to the Kakul military camp in Abbottabad.

'On the way, the truck was stopped, and the mob asked if there were any Sikhs. Some ladies helped us by lending us their dupattas. We removed our turbans and put on dupattas to look like women, and that's how we escaped.

'We spent a week at this camp, but then when trouble started there, we were shifted to the Wah camp near Rawalpindi. It was a huge camp, with about a lakh refugees from all over Pakistan. Trucks with refugees would pour in every day.'

However, Kohli noticed that most of the refugees were male. Due to the abductions and the honour killings, there was a palpable lack of women. 'Some people killed their own women. They asked them to jump into the well and die because they couldn't tolerate the mobs taking them away.'

'Every day or every other day, two or three thousand people would be taken by goods trains to India. We remained in fear about when or whether our turn would ever come. It came after about 25 days or so.' Despite the relief of getting on the train, the journey was extremely difficult right from the start—300 people were squeezed into a bogey that would normally accommodate 50. It was difficult to breathe.

Midway through their journey on the train, the group realized that something was amiss. 'We were not being taken towards Lahore, but towards Kasur. Then there was a deafening crash—the engine and the two front bogeys derailed. We realized later that the rails had been removed from the tracks. Suddenly, firing started.

'The firing went on for hours. Our goods train was without any roof, and the walls of the train were only 4-feet high, so the bullets were coming freely on top of us. We were open targets.' Kohli watched as people around him were hit and collapsed. He tried all the while to stay low and hide.

'And then just like that, the firing stopped, another engine was attached to the rear of the train and we were taken back to Wazirabad railway station. But once again, the firing started there, and went on through the night. At one point, the commander of the platoon that was guarding our train, came to us and told us that they had run out of ammunition. They said they couldn't save us anymore and that all of us would die.'

Kohli recalls the following day as divine intervention. In the morning, an angry mob was approaching the train. With no hope left, the group said a collective prayer to God, and just as they finished, they saw another train approaching. Initially worried about further attacks, their fears dissolved when Kohli's father recognized Brigadier Ayub Khan (later President of Pakistan) in the approaching train. Khan was from a village near Haripur and had a house near theirs; he was a good friend of Kohli's father.

'My father jumped from the train and shouted "Ayub save us!" He replied that he would ensure that we reached India safely. So, he put the Baloch regiment all around the train to guard us as we moved back towards Gujranwala. We spent a week at an intermediate camp there, and every day people were evacuated by about half a dozen buses. Our turn came after seven or eight days.'

On the bus journey, they encountered an angry mob coming from Amritsar. As the bus swerved and sped to avoid them, Kohli watched helplessly as fellow passengers on the roof with him fell on the roadside, with no possibility of stopping and rescuing them. He nearly fell himself and was only saved because the lack of space meant other passengers were sitting on his legs. Finally, after this harrowing journey, Kohli and his father reached Amritsar.

Here, they were also reunited with Kohli's brother, Harkishen. 'He was waiting at Amritsar. And he was in fact, in a worse situation. My father and I, we were keeping each other company, but he was alone, and he had no way of knowing if we were alive. Every train that came, he would wait and see the passengers. He used to come to the station, then go back to the Golden Temple, then come back again. There would be an announcement "the next train will arrive at such and such time", and so he would return again.'

However, the city itself was torn by cholera. 'People were dying every day, there was no cleanliness with dead bodies and rubbish all over. We came to Delhi.'

In Delhi, Kohli joined college. He completed his Bachelor's degree and then a Master's degree in Mathematics, enrolling as a refugee student.

In 1954, he was commissioned in the navy. This would pave the way for Kohli's second life. This second life would see as many near-death experiences as his perilous Partition journey, but this time on the slopes of the mighty Himalayas.

Kohli was stationed near Mumbai, and was put in charge of the Deep Sea Scouts. Though his weekdays would be regular naval duties, on weekends, he would take his scouts for long treks in the nearby hills.

As a naval officer, Kohli was entitled to a trip home as part of his benefits, but as a refugee without a clear base in India, he was told that he could choose to list any city as his hometown. Kohli decided to use this as an opportunity to see more of India. 'I took a map to my cabin and found that Darjeeling was very far away, so I thought of picking that. Then I found another small town beyond that—Shillong. So I thought of picking that. But on my way to declare it at the naval office, I remembered, that Shillong would take me further away in the other direction from my father. I wouldn't have been able to go see my father who had done so much for me, raised me as both my father and my mother. So, I looked again at the map, and saw that from Delhi a route was going up to Kashmir. So I looked within Kashmir, and saw that the small town of Pahalgam was the furthest on the northwest. So I chose that.

'On my holiday in 1955, I first stopped in Delhi for a few days to be with my father, and then continued on to Pahalgam. Once there, by chance, I met someone who was going for an Amarnath yatra.'

On a whim, Kohli decided to join in. Without training or adequate gear, Kohli survived the difficult trekking and weather conditions. This would be his initiation to the Himalayas, and he knew he was hooked.

Mount Everest had just recently been summitted in 1953 by Edmund Hillary and Tenzing Norgay, and the government had set up the Himalayan Mountaineering Institute in Darjeeling in 1954 to encourage mountaineering. 'I enrolled in its first course,' he says.

Soon after, in 1956, Kohli received an invitation to join an expedition to Saser Kangri in Ladakh. Though the group could not summit Saser Kangri, Kohli summited a 21,000-foot peak solo, setting the first steps for a record-breaking mountaineering path ahead.

The following year, he led a naval trek to Nanda Kot (22,510 feet). The group faced treacherous conditions en route, including days of almost zero visibility. But despite this, he and a colleague triumphantly managed to summit and plant the Indian flag and naval ensign. In 1961, he led a team that successfully summitted the last of the Annapurna peaks despite avalanches and heavy snowfall.

The peak that still eluded him was Mount Everest. In 1962, he made his second attempt at summitting Everest. He had three near-death experiences. The first was when they were forced to ration their oxygen use, spending three nights at over 27,000 feet with very limited oxygen, because of weather delays. The second was when one of his team members, to whom he was roped, slipped, almost resulting in a deadly 10,000-feet fall. The third was when after a long unsuccessful summit attempt, they lost their way in a blizzard and then the ensuing nightfall, giving up all hope of finding their tent; they stumbled on it only by accident at 10 p.m. Thus, though the group was unsuccessful in their summit, their mere survival and return was a commendable feat.

But these attempts only gave Kohli further drive to join the final Indian summit attempt in 1965. Kohli set a world record that year of putting a total of nine men atop the world's highest peak on 20, 22, 24 and 29 May. The team was joyously welcomed by the Prime Minister of India on their return. They received three Padma Bhushans and eight Padma Shris for this achievement. The entire team also received the Arjuna award, India's highest sporting honour. Indira Gandhi later called the expedition 'a masterpiece of planning, organization, teamwork, individual effort and leadership.'

For Kohli, the mountains became a way of life. He went on to promote responsible adventure tourism in the Himalayas, and also set up the Himalayan Environmental Trust to prevent their degradation. He steered the Indian Mountaineering Foundation as President/Vice President for 14 years.

From a young boy, who almost could not escape the violence of Partition, Kohli went on to battle the world's toughest conditions, and to survive and triumph.

A Refugee Who Built a Business Empire

Dharampal Gulati

Born: 27 March 1923 in Sialkot, undivided Punjab
(now in Pakistan)

Dharampal Gulati is perhaps the most recognized grandfather on Indian television, as he appears regularly in the advertisements for his company, MDH Masalas. A fifth-class dropout, Dharampal has outwitted the CEOs of other consumer goods companies to create a spice empire valued at around ₹1,000 crore.

Ninety-five-year-old Dharampal Gulati is amongst the highest paid Chief Executives in India, according to newspaper reports from early 2017, which pegged his salary at ₹21 crores in the previous year. He did not, however, start his life in easy circumstances. The roughly ₹1,000-crore masala empire he has built has been a result of his sheer business acumen and perseverance.

He was born in Sialkot (now in Pakistan) on 27 March 1923 to Chunnilal Gulati and Channan Devi. Living in a joint family, with two brothers, five sisters and seven cousins, Dharampal remembers a childhood of much love and play. It was a down-to-earth, rustic life as the family was not very wealthy. Dharampal remembers taking care of the two buffaloes, mornings at the akhada (wrestling ring) and the joy of eating his mother's home-cooked food.

At age five, he was enrolled in the local Arya Samaj school. But he was not very interested in studies and dropped out of school of his own will at a young age. 'I could never concentrate on my studies.' He recalls an incident from the fifth class when his English teacher pinched him for not knowing the answer to a question—for Dharampal, that was the end of his formal education. 'I decided that studying is very difficult and I didn't go back to school from the next day.' He had not even taken his fifth class examination.

'I used to play, I used to fly kites and pigeons and slowly I got older. My father asked me, "What will you do? How do you plan to become successful in life?"' Dharampal started experimenting with different trades. He tried carpentry, soapmaking, working with glass, cloth trading, working with a goldsmith, but he couldn't stick with anything.

The family business was spices. Dharampal started working

in the shop that his father jointly ran with his brother. The shop was called 'Mahashian di Hatti', and it was in a local market called Bazaar Pansaariyaan in Sialkot. He would help out with everything, making packets of spices, or taking small pouches of mehndi for door-to-door sales. The family was renowned for a special spice—deggi mirch—and Dharampal took on the role of salesperson. 'I went to Wazirabad, Majitha... I expanded the business to Lahore. From Lahore, we expanded to Sheikhupura and after that to Nankana Sahib, then to Lyallpur and then till Multan.' The shop's sales grew rapidly, and Dharampal recalls that sales reached between ₹500–800 per day—a large sum in those days.

At one point, Dharampal's father, Chunnilal, helped to set up a shop for Dharampal and his brother, Satpal. However, the location of the shop was such that it proved economically unviable. They ultimately shut it down.

Around this time, in 1942, Dharampal got married at age 18 to Leelavati. Tragedy would strike the young couple when their first two children passed away as infants. Little did they know the many challenges fate was still going to throw their way.

Life then still consisted of simple pleasures. Dharampal remembers the excitement when during World War II, a neighbour got a radio. The entire neighbourhood would gather in this person's house to hear the news on this still-rare contraption. However, soon they would hear much grimmer news close to home.

Dharampal and his family had no idea that they would have to leave their own land and home to go to a new city with which they had no ties, where they knew no one, where the way of speaking, the culture, the customs would all be different. It is very difficult for a family of ordinary means to think about leaving their ancestral home and their business. However, the escalating riots in Sialkot in 1947 made it impossible to stay. 'Every night we heard the shouts of *Allah hu Akbar, Har Har Mahadev.*' Then one day, their neighbour's house was set on fire by a mob. Some people came to Dharampal's father and advised him to leave. On the night of 14 August 1947, instead of the fireworks of celebration, the family could see the orange glow of so many homes and businesses going up in flames. For families that had spent a lifetime building their factories and homes, to lose everything overnight was devastating.

On 20 August 1947, the family moved to a refugee camp. 'We didn't bring anything, just a little money,' remembers Dharampal. They had given their buffalo to their Muslim tailor, who in turn helped them recover some cash lying at their shop.

A few weeks later, on 7 September, as the situation got worse, they decided to leave the camp for Amritsar. They managed to get to the railway station in Sialkot on a military truck, and from there took a train the following morning for Amritsar. As the train passed stations like Pasroor and Narowal, they could see mobs gathered, and their fear kept rising. Finally, they reached the border town of Jassar, across the Ravi river from Dera Baba Nanak. At the river, the stench of corpses was unbearable; everywhere around them was death. 'Our train reached safely but in the train that came behind us, everyone was killed.' In the pouring rain, with great difficulty, the family crossed the bridge on the river Ravi, moving finally from Pakistan to India.

That night a grievous tragedy befell them. While they were sleeping near the railway tracks, a military truck accidentally drove over his uncle's leg. 'His leg broke. We spent the night crying.' In the middle of the night, in an unknown place, the family was at a loss to know what to do. They managed to make their way to a nearby hospital, but realized that there were no medicines or doctors there. Fortunately, the following morning a truck from Amritsar came bearing food for the refugees, and the family was able to transport their uncle on this truck to the Civil Hospital in Amritsar.

The fracture was severe—the doctors had to put both steel implants and weights inside to straighten it. His leg was also put in a plaster. It would eventually take more than three months for his leg to heal.

By 27 September, Dharampal realized that it was difficult to find work in Amritsar. He and two of his relatives decided to go to Delhi, while the rest stayed back in Amritsar with their injured uncle. Their train to Jalandhar stopped midway as a bridge had been washed away due to the heavy monsoons. They made their way partly on foot, partly by truck to Ludhiana, where they found some relatives who had also come from across the border, and who were now staying in a house evacuated by a Muslim family. The following morning, they left for Delhi to find one of Dharampal's sisters, who was in Delhi as her husband had a government job. Dharampal remembers the mayhem: 'People were sitting on the roofs of trains because there was no space inside, but none of them knew that there were so many tunnels—a lot of them fell off when the train would go through tunnels. They died. The train was moving very slowly and we reached Sabzi Mandi station in Delhi at 4 a.m. the next morning. I had only ₹1,500 in my pocket,' he remembers.

Dharampal had heard of Delhi many times on the radio but he had never been there. They got off at the railway station and made their way on foot to Karol Bagh to find his sister. She had managed to claim one of the abandoned houses in that area for them—a broken down, ramshackle place. 'It was a small house with hardly any place to sleep. There was no running water, no latrine.' Staying in this place was difficult, especially given the heavy rains that seeped through the broken roof areas into the room. But it was a shelter nonetheless. Dharampal and his two relatives moved in there.

Dharampal remembers that it was here in Delhi that he heard his new moniker—'refugee'. He went to the government office and registered the family details, and in return was given a refugee card that entitled them to basic rations.

'I was wondering what I should do... One day, while roaming around, I reached Chandni Chowk. People were selling tangas (horse carriages) there. I asked them how much they were selling for. I bargained a little bit and finally got a tanga for ₹650.' Dharampal had decided that he would try to earn his livelihood as a tanga driver, while also taking the opportunity to acquaint himself with his new hometown. 'I used to wait near the railway station and say "two annas sawari, two annas". I would observe the other tangawallahs and then shout out neighbourhood names, like "Karol Bagh, two annas, Karol Bagh, two annas". However, Dharampal soon realized that he was not enjoying this new profession. He found the other tangawallahs uncouth, and the work draining, with little monetary reward.

He then tried opening a small stall to sell cane sugar, but he saw no prospects in this either, and soon shut it down.

More and more relatives started arriving, particularly his parents and the rest of the family who had stayed back in Amritsar to be with his uncle till the leg healed. Their little house was soon overflowing with extended family members, but they could not turn anyone away.

The family was struggling to make ends meet. Despite an

initial hesitation about going back to spice trading, Dharampal soon realized that this was the trade they knew best and that could help them find their feet again.

They started with a small wooden roadside shop.

Life was tough. Dharampal remembers that the lack of a latrine in the house meant that they would have to queue up each morning at a public municipal latrine. The family had to live frugally, especially given the large extended family that had joined.

To grow the business, he put an ad in a popular Hindi newspaper, *Pratap*—'*Mahashian di Hatti of Sialkot Deggi Mirch Waale*'.

This proved to be a winning solution. Within days, they started getting numerous orders by mail. One of the first was all the way from Cuttack in Odisha from a businessman who had migrated from Multan.

The business started growing. Dharampal decided to open one more shop in the main spice market in Delhi, Khari Baoli, and then soon another. Meanwhile, they had also put in a claim with the Ministry of Rehabilitation for the shop and property that they had left behind in Sialkot. They were allotted a plot in Gaffar Market.

Dharampal would work 12 to 15 hours a day to ensure that the business could establish itself and grow. These long hours put a strain on his health. By 1952, he had developed sciatica. The pain was so intense that for many months, he was almost completely bedridden. But he persevered.

Throughout this time, Dharampal put a strong focus on ensuring a high quality of his products. In a new city, with no business relationships, or known suppliers, he had to struggle to find the right partners. He went through quite a few bad experiences—for example, he discovered one of his suppliers was adulterating his spices with lentils to lower costs. Dharampal immediately broke the business relationship; he was quite clear that standards had to be fully maintained and exceeded. He also had the novel idea in 1949 of packaging spices in well-designed boxes. Some of the designs created in 1949 last to this day.

By 1954, the business had grown enough that the family could afford to buy their own house. This was just the start of a long journey that would see Dharampal establish his own factory in the 1960s, and go on to achieve milestone after milestone in business growth. Today, the MDH empire is valued to be around ₹1,000 crore.

From a child who dropped out of school at an early age, Dharampal went on to compete with and outmanoeuvre the highly educated CEOs of many consumer goods multinational companies.

Philanthropy has played a major part in Dharampal's life for decades, and he supports a large number of schools and hospitals.

Dharampal believes that ultimately man makes his own fate. In his autobiography, he writes, 'We ourselves are responsible for our victory or defeat, so rather than blaming fate, we should focus on cultivating our strengths and reducing our weaknesses so that this God-given mind and body can be put to full use, so that we know that all our talents and energies are doing some good in the world.'*

---

*Translation from his autobiography, *Tangaywala Kaise Bana Masalon ka Shehenshah*, [How a Tangawallah Became the King of Spices] published in Hindi by the Mahashay Chunnilal Charitable Trust.

To Look Back or to Look Ahead?

Faqir Chand Kohli

Born: 28 February 1924 in Peshawar, North-West Frontier
Province (now Khyber Pakhtunkhwa province in Pakistan)

*Faqir Chand Kohli is often credited as the 'Father of the Indian
Software Industry'. He was one of the earliest pioneers in the country
to bring the use of computers across many industries, including
power generation. He was the founding General Manager of Tata
Consultancy Services (TCS), which recently became the second listed
Indian company to cross $1 billion in market capitalization. Faqir
Chand has been awarded the Padma Bhushan (2002), apart from
many lifetime achievement awards and honorary doctorates.*

'I was born in Peshawar, where my family owned a department store. It was a large store with about a hundred employees. We supplied clothing to the British Army and civilians. We used to export to the UK. Business was thriving, so we did not have any problems as such. I had three older brothers—they were all more than a decade older than me, and they also worked in the store. We lived in the quiet cantonment area,' recalls Faqir Chand.

Almost six decades later, well after Partition, Faqir Chand went back to Peshawar: 'I couldn't find my old house. But I visited the shop. It had been divided into about seven smaller parts. The people there were very nice to me, they asked me to have a meal with them, to spend time with them—it was as if I was one of their own.'

But in the 1920s and 1930s, growing up in Peshawar, Faqir Chand could never have imagined that the family would have to flee their home and a comfortable life. At that time, he was only focussed on his studies, where he always tried to excel. He first studied in the local Khalsa school and then went to the National High School, Peshawar for grades 9 and 10. 'In 1939, after I completed my matriculation, I went to do my BA (Hons) and BSc (Hons) from Government College, Lahore. I was there till 1945.'

He recalls both Peshawar and Lahore as having integrated communities. 'Both in my school and at Government College, we never felt any differences amongst the communities or like we did not belong there. In the hostel where I stayed for the first two years in Lahore, on my left was a Muslim and on my right was a Muslim. There were no problems between the different communities.

'After graduation, I was selected for a commission in the Navy in 1945, but shortly after that, within a month, I received a scholarship from the Government of India to study abroad. I had to wait till 1946 to get a ship berth to go to the United States because most ships were still commandeered for the war efforts. It took me around a month from Calcutta to San Francisco by ship.'

From 1946 to 1951, Faqir Chand was in Canada and the US. 'I had wanted to study Power [Electric] Engineering, so I went to Queen's University in Ontario, Canada, which was ranked number one in that field. After that, I worked with the Canadian General Electric Company for a year.'

Faqir Chand was still in Canada on Independence Day in 1947. 'There were hardly any Indians in Canada, so there wasn't much one could do to celebrate,' he recalls.

'I then went to MIT in Cambridge [Massachusetts, USA] for a master's degree. When I graduated from MIT, I got an offer from the Tata Group to help them set up a Load Dispatch system, which is where we decide how much power a given power station can generate efficiently. So, I spent about six months working in the US at the New England Power System learning how they managed their Load Dispatch, and then I came back to India. I already had an offer from MIT to continue on to a PhD, so my thinking was that I would see what the Tata job was like here, and if I didn't like it, I would go back to MIT.

'But when I came back in 1951, and joined my family in Lucknow, what I found was so distressing that I never even considered going back.' He found his family's circumstances completely transformed. 'We were so prosperous in Peshawar, but here in Lucknow, my family was sleeping on the ground.

I cried a lot that first night I saw them. I decided that I am not going back to the US but would stay with my family.'

While he had been in Canada, Faqir Chand had not fully understood the devastation that Partition had wreaked on his family. 'They just told me that they were moving to Lucknow, that is all. They told me not to worry, and to continue with my studies. They did not tell me what condition they were in. I only found out when I came back.'

Before he had left for Canada in 1946, though there had been some talk of Pakistan, it had not seemed like it would ever materialize. 'I couldn't have imagined that the country would be partitioned. I had left a single country—I took a train from Peshawar to Calcutta and a ship from Calcutta to San Francisco.' But by the time he returned in 1951, the borders had been very firmly drawn between two nation-states. There was no question of returning to Peshawar.

'When the ship docked in Bombay in 1951, two of my brothers received me there, and took me to Lucknow. They had all migrated to Lucknow during Partition, except for one brother who went to Kanpur.

'I never spoke to my family about Partition, or how they had made their way to Lucknow. Partition had been so very painful for them, and I did not want them to recall that painful time. I could not have done anything to change the past.' Instead, Faqir Chand focussed on changing their future. 'We did not receive any compensation from the government. We had lost everything.' He felt a weight of responsibility in helping the family to find economic security again. He focussed on building a solid career. He took up the job with Tata Electric (now Tata Power).

The systems Faqir Chand set in place at Tata Electric were

based on what he had seen abroad. These put the Tata Group at an advantage in the Indian market as they were able to reduce power losses considerably. 'This ensured continuity and reliability of our supply, and we could also pass some savings to our consumers.'

Faqir Chand also brought a number of advanced computing technologies to their work. 'In 1964, the first computer came to India and was installed at the Tata Institute of Fundamental Research. We started using it for our technical calculations. In 1968, we went even further—installing a computer that helped us control the grid between Bombay to Pune. It told us what was happening at every generating station from minute to minute. This was really pioneering work. Back then, most systems in the UK, Europe and Japan were still on analogue systems; only a few utilities in the USA used modern computers.'

His advanced expertise and methods were noticed within the company. He was rapidly promoted to positions with more and more responsibility. 'When they wanted to set up a company in computers, they asked me to head it, and that is how I came to TCS.' In September 1969, Faqir Chand joined the newly opened Tata Consultancy Services as General Manager.

His task was to establish and grow this fledgling software company in a country where computers were few and far between. The socialist economic policies of the government and the strong labour unions meant high tariffs and a lot of restrictions on the use of mainframe computers, which were viewed as direct threats to jobs. Faqir Chand managed to purchase a mainframe at a fraction of the original price from a state-owned insurance company that had been blocked from using it by their labour union.

A few years later in 1974, upon the death of the Director,

Faqir Chand was made the Director-in-Charge of TCS. This would be a role he would hold for two decades till 1994, during which time he would grow TCS into one of the largest companies in India, and one of the largest software companies in the world.

But in the 1970s, Faqir Chand had to work hard to find clients for TCS both within and outside India. They managed to successfully deliver on complex problems like inter-branch reconciliation for the banking system. They also worked on Bombay's (now Mumbai) telephone exchange. But the real growth came when Faqir Chand was able to break into the foreign market bringing on clients like Burroughs, then one of the largest computer manufacturers in the US. At a time when no one was using the term 'outsourcing', Faqir Chand kickstarted the Indian outsourcing industry.

Today, TCS is one of the largest companies in India by market capitalization. In April 2018, it became only the second listed Indian company ever (after Reliance Industries) to cross a $100 billion market capitalization. It has been recognized by Forbes for its innovation. It generates some two-thirds of the dividends of its parent company, Tata Sons. It has almost 300 offices across more than forty countries and is the fourth largest employer in India.

Though Faqir Chand retired from TCS in 1999, he has not really retired at all. At 94, he still goes to office most days, and spends his time building IT solutions to the country's most pressing challenges.

In 1958–59 he got involved in higher education, by helping P.K. Kelkar's work on establishing IIT Bombay and IIT Kanpur. Now, post-retirement, in 2000, he was distressed to learn about the opposite end of the spectrum of education—

the high rates of adult illiteracy in India. He teamed up with linguists to understand the core of literacy. Once he realized that adults only need an average of 500 words to be able to read a newspaper, he led a team of programmers to build a software solution that used images to teach adults complete words rather than focus on the alphabet. Within a decade, the project had helped over 1,20,000 adults become functionally literate in their own native language.

He now believes that the next wave of software development in India needs to be natively developed in Indian languages. 'There are 700 to 800 million people in this country, who don't speak English. We need to develop India-specific applications for them.'

For his efforts, Kohli has received numerous awards and recognitions. These include the Padma Bhushan (2002), and Lifetime Achievement Awards from *The Economic Times* (2002), All India Management Association (2002) and Indian National Academy of Engineering (2000).

He has also received many honorary doctorates over the course of his life, including ones from the University of Waterloo, Canada (1990), Robert Gordon University, Aberdeen, UK (2000), IIT Bombay (2004) and IIT Kanpur (2006), among others. Decades earlier, Faqir Chand had eschewed pursuing his doctoral degree in the US so he could instead focus on supporting his family post-Partition. Now, life has come full circle with all these honorary doctorates. Even though his family had lost everything, Faqir Chand never looked back or questioned what had happened; he looked forward and charted a new course, not just for his family, but for the country.

Jijibisha: The Will to Survive

Manoranjan Byapari

Born: 1950, Barisal, East Pakistan (now in Bangladesh)

Manoranjan Byapari learnt how to read in his twenties while in jail in West Bengal. Today, he is the published author of over 100 short stories and 10 books. He is perhaps the only former convict-turned-rickshaw-puller-turned-cook to have reached such literary heights. He has been published by Oxford University Press and Economic and Political Weekly, amongst others. He was awarded the Suprabha Majumdar prize by the Paschimbanga Bangla Akademi (2015) for his writings.

'Two categories of people came from East Pakistan to present-day West Bengal,' begins Manoranjan Byapari. 'The first were the upper-caste people and the other the lower-caste people. I was born in East Pakistan's Barisal district in a family that some might refer to as "impure" or "untouchable". Before 1911, we were known as the "chandalas" and presently we are known as the "namasudras".

'The government and political parties are all made of the upper-caste people, so they have looked after their own interests. They knew about the Partition of the country before 1947, so they sold or exchanged their lands, exchanged their jobs and shifted to West Bengal in 1947. But, we belonged to the lower castes, individuals with no property; all we could do was work. We had no option other than working hard and surviving. We could not accept or imagine being displaced from our land and livelihoods. This is the reason why we came later to this side of Bengal.' Manoranjan's family only moved in 1953, as part of the large Namasudra migration of the early 1950s when over a million Dalits moved from East Pakistan to India.

Manoranjan was three years old at that time. He does not remember the journey itself due to his age, but the tough refugee life that lay ahead seared itself in the mind of the young child.

'When we came to this side of Bengal, we were kept in refugee camps at the Shiromanipur camp in Bankura. We lived there for roughly seven years, but then one day, we were told that we cannot live in Bengal and we had to move to Dandakaranya because the government could not provide us any place in Bengal.' Dandakaranya is the forest area now shared between Chhattisgarh and neighbouring states like

53

Odisha and Andhra Pradesh. 'Most people's only association with Dandakaranya is from the Ramayana, where this forest is the residence of rakshasas (demons). So we were reluctant to shift there.

'But once we said no to going there, the government stopped helping us in any way. Their attitude was "if you do not want to go to Dandakaranya, then it is not my responsibility to look after you". Without government support, families began to starve. They had no shelter. They just found any space they could in Kolkata—beside rail tracks, slums, canals—and struggled to survive. They tried to find work as wage labourers, cleaners and so on. We migrated to a camp near Ghutiyari Sharif called Gholadoltala in South 24 Parganas.'

Life was very tough for Manoranjan and the countless other families like his who had no support or means of sustaining themselves. They often sustained themselves on just a thin broth made by boiling cheap chicken feed—the only thing they could afford.

'Some years later, my father was working in Jadavpur as a daily labourer. He did not have money to pay for the train ticket, so he used to leave home early in the morning before the ticket collectors came to duty and used to wait till the evening when the collectors left from duty. If on a given day he found work, then he would eat, otherwise he would just sit the whole day without eating any food because he did not have enough money to even feed himself. This eventually affected his health and led to gastric ulcer. The only earning member of our house was bedridden. Thus, no income led to intense starvation in our house.'

Manoranjan could not bear the shadow of hunger that hung constantly on the family. He recalls his younger siblings crying from hunger, desperate for even a little bit of rice or broth; a hunger so deep that it was overpowering. His younger sister passed away from starvation. The pall of gloom hung heavier. Manoranjan decided to run away from home. He was around 14 years old at that time.

He boarded a train to New Jalpaiguri and started working at a tea stall on the station. The owner had agreed to pay him ₹40 a month; however, months came and went, and every time Manoranjan asked, he was told that he would be paid the following month. After eight months of such exploitation without pay, Manoranjan decided to find work somewhere else. He went to Guwahati. After six months, he had saved up nearly ₹200. But the world was still exploiting the young child. This money, too, was stolen from him; he suspects, by his employers themselves. He then went to Lucknow. This would be the worst exploitation yet. He was taken in by a policeman on the pretext of working in his home as a cook and was sexually abused.

Manoranjan continued to drift to different cities to find work—Kanpur, Delhi, Allahabad, Haridwar, Mathura, Vrindavan. 'I travelled all across India. If I managed to find work, I would work; if I couldn't, then I would not eat, I would just drink water that day. Sometimes, when I was starving and couldn't control my hunger, I would steal bread and run away.

'I did not have a childhood like most people. I was never able to buy kites or any kind of toys. I never played with colours. During festivals, I used to be very sad because everyone else wore new clothes but my trousers were torn and I had to cover them with my hands. This is how my childhood days were spent. I never went to school. My father did not have any money to buy me books or pens or even a slate. I wanted to live

Jijibisha: The Will to Survive

my life honestly and peacefully but I never got an opportunity to do so.'

Manoranjan's family had, in the meanwhile, moved from Gholadoltala to Jadavpur in the hope that his mother and grandmother could work as domestic help and supplement the family income. Between them, they were able to earn ₹22 a month, adding substantially to ₹1–2 that his father earned every day from working in a ration shop. In 1969, Manoranjan also came to Jadavpur. However, with no earnings to offer them for all his time away, Manoranjan was too ashamed to stay with them. That shame was pivotal in him joining some local goons; he learnt how to wield a knife.

In 1969, the Naxalbari movement was gaining momentum in Bengal. 'I had started working as a daily labourer. One day, I did not have any work to do and I was having a conversation with a few boys regarding Naxalbari. I was sharing stories with them about Jungle Santhal [a leader of the Naxal movement]. I told them that I had seen Jungle Santhal, even though I hadn't. I simply made up some stories but listening to my stories one person got so inspired that he wanted to become a Naxalite. The place where we were sitting was next to a kali temple. This boy picked up a piece of charred wood, and on the wall where it was written CPI(M), he added an L making it CPI(ML) [the Naxalite party]. One passerby witnessed all this and reported it in the CPI(M) party office.

'That evening, the CPI(M) workers came and took me with them. They tied me to a lamp post and beat me up really badly. Their main aim was to give a message to the local youth and residents that if one tries to become a part of this revolt then one will get beaten up like this. The person who wrote on the wall was not hurt because his father had a grocery shop.

He had four brothers, he was a local, and he also belonged to the Kshatriya caste; whereas I was from an untouchable and impure caste. We came from outside for work; my mother worked as a maid, my father and I were both daily labourers. I was an appropriate target for them.'

Manoranjan did in fact get involved with the Naxal movement. However, soon with the war of 1971, a flood of refugees arrived in West Bengal, and amongst them was Manoranjan's uncle who had stayed back in East Pakistan till then. He advised Manoranjan's father to move the family to Dandakaranya. 'My family and I moved to Dandakaranya, we cut wood and built a thatched hut for ourselves. But it was very difficult to stay there. There was no water, the heat was unbearable and the environment was generally unfriendly. The bus stop was 25 km away and the railway station was 200 km away from the place. We were stuck inside a deep jungle. After two years there, I came back to Jadavpur in 1973.'

He started driving a rickshaw. He was only 23 then, but life had thrown innumerable obstacles in his way. Exploited repeatedly, the young man had learnt that toughness was needed to survive in the world he lived in.

'I started to carry passengers to and from Jadavpur station. I used to get drunk every day, pick a fight at any time, collect protection money from illicit liquor sellers. The sex workers used to take their customers to the deserted goods trains, so we would mug them and take away their belongings. I was finally arrested for living like this. The day I was put inside the jail, I met a man who must have been 55 or 56 years old and had been held under a cheating case. He told me to get educated. He brought a twig and taught me the Bengali alphabet by writing with it on the floor. One day, while I was practising, I caught the attention of a policeman. This effort of mine had somehow struck a chord in him. Those days, it was against the rules to provide an undertrial with a pen and a paper but because of the policeman's insistence, the jailor made an exception. And that's how I learnt to read and write, inside the prison.'*

Manoranjan had gone to jail in 1975. In two years, he had been in three jails—Alipore Special Jail, Central Jail and Presidency Jail. Life had hit its lowest point. But finally, the young man—still only 27—was going to start seeing better days.

'When I came out of prison after 26 months, I knew how to read. In fact, I was now addicted to one thing—reading books. I could not leave this habit. I would read sitting under the tree, or while waiting for a passenger for my rickshaw. I never wasted a single minute. Through books, I could know everything: about the top of the highest mountain in the Himalayas, or the bottom of the deepest ocean, about space, about Africa. I could know all this without leaving my home.'

Manoranjan started buying as many books as he could afford; often going to junk stores where they were sold by weight. He was entranced by the worlds and lives they could take him to, so different from the tough life he had known.

'One day, I couldn't find the meaning of a difficult word I was reading, "jijibisha". A passenger sat in my rickshaw and I asked her the meaning of this word. She was amazed by the fact that a rickshaw-puller knew such a difficult word. She asked me where I had learnt this word, to which I replied that I read it in a book. So she asked me which books I had read

*Interview by Rajya Sabha TV, 2014.

and I named some 10–15 books that I had recently read. She told me the meaning of the word is "the will to survive". Then she asked if I would like to write in a magazine. When she got down, she gave her contact information, and that's when I realized that it was the author, Mahasweta Devi.'

This pivotal moment would change Manoranjan's life. Mahasweta Devi was already an acclaimed writer by then, and she was editor of a magazine called, *Bartika*. Manoranjan's first piece was published in this magazine in early 1981; it was titled 'Rickshaw Chalai' (I Pull a Rickshaw).

His writing was noticed. 'An article came out in a newspaper and so some Jadavpur University professors started looking for me. Soon, several magazines and newspapers started asking for my work. Many people came to me and asked me to write for them regarding my life during my prison term, my travel experiences across India without ticket, and my experience in camps. This is how I eventually established myself as a writer.'

Manoranjan slowly thus built a strong space in the Bengali literary world. Because his works were steeped in his own experiences as a Dalit and looked at the hardships and injustices faced by marginalized populations, he came to be known as the pioneer of Dalit Bengali literature.

He came to national prominence with the publication of an essay called 'Is there Dalit Writing in Bangla?' in the 13 October 2007 issue of the journal *Economic and Political Weekly*. (It was translated by Meenakshi Mukherjee.)

The translation of his autobiography (*Itibritte Chandal Jiban*, 2012) into English (*Interrogating My Chandal Life: An Autobiography of a Dalit*, 2016) brought him even further into the limelight nationally. However, it has not changed his financial condition. He is still dependent on working as a cook in a school to support himself financially. In his life, Manoranjan has worked at a tea stall, in a crematorium, as a cook, as a sweeper, as manual labour, as a guard, a rickshaw-puller, a cowherd, amongst other things. But for the young boy who never really had a childhood, his writings have allowed him to find his place in the world.

Still he does not feel at ease; in fact, it is this unease that propels his writing. 'I do not have my own country,' he says. 'I am "desh-bhikhari". If I go back to the other side of Bengal—even though I have never returned since I do not have a passport, but I have heard stories from people who travel to the other side—we are known as kaafir, malaon, bidharmi, Hindu. And yet, when I am on this side of Bengal, I am known as bastuhara, udbastu, refugee, saronharti, boiragoto, gonoprobeshkari and bangal. (That is, on the other side, we are called non-believers or someone outside the faith, and on this side, we are called refugees or outsiders.) I do not have my own country. This partition of the country took away my country from me. If Partition hadn't happened, we would have at least had some land, a house and a river.'

How Will You Partition the Air?

Gulzar

Born: 18 August 1936 in Dina, Jhelum district,
undivided Punjab (now in Pakistan)

Gulzar is one of India's most eminent poets. His evocative words have given voice to the emotions of millions of Indians through his film lyrics and scripts, short plays and poems. He received the Academy Award and a Grammy Award for his lyrics to 'Jai Ho' from Slumdog Millionaire, as well as, numerous awards in India, including the Padma Bhushan, Sahitya Akademi award, Dadasaheb Phalke award, and over 20 Filmfare awards and National Film awards.

'For 20 or 25 years after Partition, I would keep having nightmares of the riots. These bad dreams would come regularly at night. I would wake up tense, and then I couldn't go back to sleep. That fear was there, a terror, that if I went back to sleep, I'd have the same nightmare again,' recalls Gulzar.

Born in Dina in Jhelum district in, what is now Pakistan, Gulzar was already living in Delhi at the time of the Partition. Though he didn't have to flee in a kaafila or a train, he still witnessed the worst of Partition violence, watching his neighbourhood descend into frenzied riots.

The family was living near Subzi Mandi in Basti Punjabia, a neighbourhood in Old Delhi. It was a mixed, Muslim-majority neighbourhood, and many of Gulzar's friends and classmates were Muslim.

Few would realize that the master of Urdu poetry, Gulzar, was not born with that name. His name is so closely intertwined with our idea of him, with the beautiful shayari from films like *Aandhi* and *Mausam*, which poignantly touch the heart of our emotions, that we cannot imagine him being known by any other name. But Gulzar actually grew up as Sampooran Singh Kalra. Born in a Sikh household to Makhan Singh Kalra and Sajjan Kaur, Gulzar followed the traditional Sikh custom of keeping long hair, when he was young.

At the time of Partition, the young Sikh boy was 11 years old. Old enough that the agonizing images of the corpses lining the streets were seared into his memory.

'We saw half-burnt dead bodies on the roads in front of our house, on the entire road. The road near Roshanara Bagh is really big, and it was covered with corpses. These included bodies of people known to me. I recognized them, I had played marbles with them; they were there, their fathers were also lying there.

'Someone with a half-burnt arm, someone with a half-burnt leg. And the bodies slowly started decomposing because no one was there to clear the corpses.

'An unbearable stench spread around the entire area. People put chairs and beds on the corpses and put kerosene oil on them and burnt the corpses, some burnt people alive. The remains were put on trucks and taken away. How can we forget it?'

The family had moved into a compound for safety. The municipal middle school Gulzar studied in had shut down. 'People were so worried, they all got together in a compound, no one wanted to stay home alone because there was always a fear that they would be attacked. Going to that compound required walking past these corpses. Some of the charred remains were stuck to the road, they had to be scraped off. The half-burnt houses were everywhere.

'There was one Muslim boy in school particularly, who used to, I remember, lead the prayers in school. He was senior to me in school—a very fair boy, very musically talented. One day I saw a man, I later got to know his name was Samandar Singh, dragging this young boy away. The boy was just going meekly, he wasn't even protesting. When he took him away, I cried all night, I remember. We knew he was taking the boy behind Roshanara Bagh to kill him.'*

These experiences shaped and scarred Gulzar immensely. 'I must thank my father for his broad mindedness that we

---

*'Partition through the eyes of Indian Authors: Gulzar', a presentation by IGNOU, produced by Factual Media Network, research and script by Sukrita Paul Kumar.

didn't grow bitter, despite the fact that he lost so much at that time—money, property, relatives...'[*] The nightmares stayed with Gulzar and haunted him. It was only decades later that his writing helped him overcome the fears.

'Learning how to write had this one advantage, that I could purge it out. It was a way I could cope with the nightmares. Something that had become solid inside me, had been so firmly imprinted in me, began to loosen and I could purge it out.'

Many short stories and poems have come out of this process of purging. 'Bhamiri' beautifully captures the lost innocence of childhood, 'Dastak' the destruction of dreams. His poignant story 'Ravi Paar' portrays the agony of losing a child and some part of oneself: 'A lady arrived at a camp with a dead child, she was clinging to it dearly, and would not let go of it. That image stayed with me. I could identify with this woman—the idea that Partition also left some part of me dead. That whatever was thrown away was the life in me. So that idea took shape over the years and became the story of "Ravi Paar". Gulzar combined different incidents from his memory into his stories: 'The story called "Jamun ka Ped" did not happen exactly in that particular manner, rather different incidents were combined and compounded. So, the experience of three families becomes the experience of one family. But many of the characters are real—the characters of Ahmed, Dina and the old woman are all based on real people.'[†]

The story of *Batwara* is also Gulzar's own experience of Partition, albeit from much later. '*Batwara* is the story about a gentleman who thought I was his lost son. The way it happened

[*]Ibid.
[†]Ibid.

to me is what I've written exactly. The names in the story are their real names. It is a very long story. In the days of the Janata government [late 1970s] in Punjab, there was a minister, Harbhajan Singh, who was convinced that I am his long-lost son. What had happened is that during Partition, while fleeing, he had lost one son and one daughter who were left behind. When the violence started increasing, the local landlord told Harbhajan Singh that he would give them shelter. He was a close friend of the family, and he had made them swear that they would let him help them and shelter them. But Harbhajan Singh was worried because people from outside the area had also started coming and going, and there were a lot of attacks. He was not sure if they would be safe there. So one night, without telling the landlord, the family joined a kaafila leaving the town. Somewhere near Chhoti Mianwali, there was a fear of an attack on the kaafila. In the chaos that followed, he lost his youngest son and daughter.

'Decades later, when he was visiting Pakistan in the mid-1970s, he wrote a letter to the landlord, Afzal, and the landlord's son, Ayaz. At first, he didn't have the courage to put it in the mail because he assumed that the landlord would feel that they had betrayed his trust by leaving that night, especially without telling him. But finally, just before leaving the country, Harbhajan Singh posted the letter in Karachi.'

It was eight years later that the family got a response. 'When Ayaz passed away, people came to visit him from all over. His things were being looked at, and in the pocket of his shirt his son found the letter. He mentioned it to the relatives who had come for the funeral. And, as fate would have it, one of the relatives said, "The girl you're talking about, she is actually present here today."

'Sometime later, Ayaz's son wrote to Harbhajan Singh, and Singh went to Pakistan to meet his daughter. She remembered her original name, Satya, and also remembered her parents' names. She said that that night of the kaafila in 1947, she had been feeling very sleepy, so she went behind a tandoor and slept, and when she woke up the caravan had already left. She had been taken in by a local family, converted to Islam and was now known as Dilshad. She was married with two grown-up children, one in the Air Force, and one working in a business.

'Even though it had been 40 years since they lost their children, those memories didn't fade. The fact that they had found their daughter, gave them hope to start looking again for their son. So one day I got a call that the family wanted to see me. In fact, a few different people called me. At first, I said, "no, no this is not me", "I know my parents", "I was already in Delhi during the Partition". But they were so keen, so I agreed to meet them. The whole family was there. I asked them why they thought I was their son, and they said it was because our names were the same—"Sampooran Singh", and their son was also called Poonni or Poonna, as I had been.

'Throughout the conversation, the mother—Harbhajan Singh's wife—did not say much, she was just staring at me most of the time. But a couple of times, she stopped the conversation and asked, "Why don't you just accept that you are my son?" It was very tragic, that hope still lived in her after all this time that she would find her son.

'Years later, when Harbhajan Singh passed away, I got a letter from his son, saying that "*Maa ne kaha hai ki chhotte ko bata dena*" (Mother said to let the youngest son know).

'Is this a story or is this life? What is life without stories? Stories come from life itself, where else can they come from?

And life is made of stories only. So, I have written this and it was published too and I kept everyone's original names the same.'

But all this happened many decades later after Gulzar had established himself as a leading poet, film lyricist and scriptwriter. In 1947, he was still a young student.

He completed his matriculation from a local school in Old Delhi. But the family was struggling economically. Gulzar's mother, Sajjan Kaur, had passed away when he was just a young child, and his father, Makhan Singh, had remarried. He had five children from this marriage, and an additional three from his first marriage (Sajjan Kaur was his second wife). Many relatives were also still staying with the family post-Partition. Property in Jhelum had been lost during Partition. Makhan Singh decided to send Gulzar to Bombay (now Mumbai) in August 1949 to stay with Jasmer Singh Kalra, Gulzar's eldest brother.

Jasmer had a petrochemical business in Bombay. Gulzar joined Khalsa College in Bombay. He stayed in a single-room apartment owned by his brother and started helping at his brother's petrol pump.

The young boy felt somewhat displaced in a new city, away from most of his family. But the spare time allowed him to spend time writing, watching plays and developing a love for the arts. He joined the Indian People's Theatre Association (IPTA), the Progressive Writers' Association (PWA) and the Punjabi Sahitya Sabha (PSS). Through PWA, Gulzar started meeting literary icons like Faiz Ahmed Faiz and Kaifi Azmi; through PSS, stalwarts like Balraj Sahni and Rajinder Singh Bedi.

It was around this time that Sampooran Singh Kalra, who

had already adopted the pen name Gulzar, also cut off the long hair that he had still maintained as a Sikh.

Gulzar's family was keen that he enter a conventional profession, but the idea of becoming an author and poet had taken seed in his mind. Though he was now working in an automobile garage called Vichare Motors, his literary friends pulled him increasingly in the direction of writing.

One day, fate intervened. Bimal Roy was making the film *Bandini* with S.D. Burman as the music composer and Shailendra as the lyricist. But, the latter two had an argument, and Shailendra walked out of the film. Gulzar's friends, including Shailendra himself, encouraged Gulzar to go meet Bimal Roy.

A reluctant Gulzar who had never thought of writing film songs—he viewed himself more as an author and poet—found himself suddenly writing lyrics for the soon-to-be-famous song 'Mora Gora Ang Lai Ley' in *Bandini*. Shortly after, in 1960, Bimal Roy invited Gulzar to become his assistant director. This formed the start of a strong friendship between them. Bimal became a mentor to the young Gulzar, pulling him closer and closer into the film industry, teaching him all the skills of the trade. Gulzar worked with Bimal as an assistant on films like *Kabuliwaala* and *Prem Patra*, simultaneously writing songs for these films and building his reputation as an evocative lyricist.

With Makhan Singh's death in 1961, most anchors to his childhood had weakened, Gulzar now turned to his film fraternity to be his family, looking upon Bimal Roy, and after his death, Hemant Kumar, as father figures. It was here that he would meet his soon-to-be wife, Rakhee, in 1969.

Amidst the films, Gulzar managed to also find time to put together his first book of short stories, called *Chauras Raat*, which was published in 1963, followed quickly by a book of poems called *Jaanam*, the following year.

Gulzar, the film lyricist and director, was fully established by the late 1960s with films like *Aashirwaad* and *Khamoshi* to his credit. A series of superhit films in the 1970s, like *Anand* and *Namak Haram* only cemented his reputation. There was no looking back after that.

In his entire film-making career, Gulzar has not made a film on Partition though, and doesn't think enough films on the topic have been made. 'The Second World War was extremely traumatic, but in Europe, in America, in Britain, they made films, and they purged it out. But we were not able to make films on Partition, neither in India nor in Pakistan, so it remained suppressed inside us and made us claustrophobic. Maybe if we had done this then, maybe if we had cried out completely, if we had completely let out our emotions and regretted the violence that happened, it would have been behind us today. But we kept it suppressed.'

Gulzar had in fact wanted to make a film on Partition as his first film, but he could not find the support to take it forward. Producers were still too shy of taking up this difficult subject. His script lay idle for a long time, and an intense uneasiness grew within him at what he saw as a wilful, claustrophobic silence. It was only much later, says Gulzar, when Govind Nihalani's *Tamas* came out that his unease quietened and he felt that what needed to be said on Partition, had now been said.

Gulzar only hopes now that the Partition that divided the land, does not continue to divide the people. 'Countries can be divided, land can be divided, roads can be divided, but you were dividing people, you were dividing cultures; these cannot be cut. How will you partition the air? The trees that were divided will grow again, and their shadows will fall on one side of the border in the morning, and the other side in the afternoon. There is no use in cutting shadows.'

He Slept on the Verandah to Protect Us

Hamida Habibullah

Born: 20 November 1916 in Lucknow, India

Hamida Habibullah was elected as an MLA in 1969; she became Social and Harijan Welfare Minister and then Tourism Minister in Uttar Pradesh from 1971–1974. She was a Member of Parliament in the Rajya Sabha from 1976–1982. She also led various organizations working on women and children's welfare.

Partition did not affect only those who migrated, but also those who chose to stay behind. The vast majority of India's Muslims did not migrate in 1947, but as large parts of north India spiralled into riots, many of them faced very difficult times initially.

These families had only lived in India, which they knew both as their home, and as a country where different communities had coexisted for centuries, so the question of leaving their homes and livelihoods did not arise for many of them. However, the atmosphere before and after Partition had grown so fraught that they had to find a way to manage through those turbulent times till life gained an even keel again.

Hamida Habibullah was a young married woman, and the mother of a small infant, with another expected soon, when Partition happened.

'The main problem was that we couldn't go out. News would reach us via some Sikh officers from our regiment about what happened or was said in the market on that day. One day, a Sikh officer came over. Maybe he heard something, he would not tell us; but he came early morning, and said he wanted to take our family to his house for a few days. When we demurred, he insisted on sleeping on our verandah to protect us,' remembered Hamida about the tense months after the Partition.

As Muslims, Hamida and her family faced the risk of an attack. She recalled being particularly worried for the safety of her son, who was just two years old then. Still, she usually felt protected because her husband, Enaith, was in the army, which took good care of its officers. 'When we were in Delhi, our servant, who was also Muslim, used to go to the market to get milk every day. One day, Colonel Kulwant Singh, a fellow officer, told us we should stop sending him as it was dangerous. When we tried to resist, he insisted that he would get the milk himself. Imagine a colonel in the army bringing us milk every day! You got to witness men like that in those times,' she reminisced.

The fear and inconveniences Hamida and her husband faced did not deter them though; their courageous attitude saw off the challenges—as they both rose in public life in the coming years.

Enaith rose to become the Commandant of the National Defence Academy from 1953–58 and was promoted to Major-General in 1955.

Hamida also led an active life of public service. With the support and encouragement of her pioneering mother-in-law, Inam Habibullah, Hamida started to get involved in educational activities focussed on women soon after marriage. Upon her husband's retirement in 1965, she decided to join active politics. She was elected as an MLA in 1969 in Uttar Pradesh and became a minister in the state government two years later—one of the few Muslim women to achieve such high office. This grande dame of Lucknow, who passed away in early 2018 at 102, is also remembered for her work on the education of girls. She was the president of the first college for girls in Lucknow to give degrees, the Avadh Girls Degree College, and she also furthered the work of Talimgah-e-Niswan College, which focussed on girls from low-income minority households. Through her work with organizations like SEWA and Nari Sewa Samiti, she remained deeply involved in pushing forward the empowerment of women.

Perhaps her commitment to justice and social causes came

from her family. She had been born in Lucknow in 1916 to Nawab Nazir Yar Jung, who later became the Chief Justice in Hyderabad. 'I came from a family of High Court judges. Three generations were judges—my father, his father and my great grandfather,' she said.

The only daughter, Hamida was doted on by her father and three brothers. She grew up in Hyderabad and did her education there, excelling at her coursework at Osmania University. In 1938, 22-year-old Hamida married a young, dashing officer of the army, 28-year-old Enaith Habibullah.

Enaith also came from a distinguished family. His father, Sheikh Mohammad Habibullah, was the Taluqdar of Awadh, and one of the early members of the civil services, holding the posts of Vice-Chancellor of Lucknow University and Deputy Commissioner, Saharanpur. His mother, Inam Habibullah, was the MLA from Lucknow, having recently won the 1937 elections. Enaith had three siblings—two brothers and a sister—Isha'at, Ali and Tazeen. All three were married by 1947.

One lingering impact of Partition on Hamida and Enaith was the division of this family.

When Partition happened, the situation in Punjab was so violent that families had no option but to leave their homes to save their lives, fleeing from Pakistan to India and vice versa. But for Hindus and Sikhs living in other parts of East and West Pakistan, and for Muslims living in other parts of India, the decision was often more nuanced. In 1947, Sindhi Hindus, for example, mostly believed that they would stay in Pakistan; their exodus did not start till early 1948. Most Bengali Hindus similarly believed they would stay in East Pakistan; their exodus only multiplied in the 1950s and continued for decades after. For Muslims living in the heartlands of India, the question of whether to leave for Pakistan or not was a very personal one.

Each couple within the Habibullah household took their own decision. A tragic consequence of this was separation.

Sheikh Muhammad and Inam Habibullah did not want to leave. Neither did Enaith or Hamida, but all his other siblings and their spouses chose to leave India.

'My great-grandmother, Inam Habibullah, was one of the founders of the women's wing of the Muslim League,' says Saif Habibullah, Hamida's grandson. 'She had contested and won a seat in the 1937 elections on a Muslim League ticket. But when Partition happened, she refused to leave. She said, "I didn't fight for this." Her involvement in the Muslim League was a fight for women's rights, she wasn't working for a separate nation. As you see in the movies, some women just sat down on their chaukhat and refused to leave—that was her! She sat down and said, "Nobody can remove me from here, because this is my home."'

Her son and daughter-in-law, Enaith and Hamida felt the same way.

At Partition, when everyone in the armed forces and government services—those working in the army, police, libraries, railways—was given the option of India or Pakistan, Enaith chose to serve in the Indian Army.

'We did not believe the country should be divided. My husband, Enaith, went to plead to Nehru that he should not allow Partition, that there is no difference between Hindus and Muslims,' remembered Hamida. 'I was asked to give a speech at a Muslim League election rally in 1946, but I refused. I said I could not, as I did not believe Partition should happen.'

Their son, Wajahat (a distinguished civil servant, who has served as the first Chief Information Commissioner and

He Slept on the Verandah to Protect Us

Chairman of the National Minorities Commission), has also noted that his father and other officers convinced the Prime Minister to revoke an order that decreed that Muslim officers could only stay on in India if they resigned from the army. 'It was only after they protested to the Prime Minister that the order was revoked,' he said.*

But Enaith's brother, Isha'at, chose to go to Pakistan. In his unpublished memoirs, he wrote about his early efforts to set up Pakistan Tobacco: 'At the end of September 1947, after finishing my leave, I proceeded via Delhi to Karachi by air to take up my duties...Ours was the first major foreign investment to be made in the country after Partition... In this context, I must mention that almost immediately after Partition was announced in June 1947, a message had been conveyed...that it was the wish of the Quaid-e-Azam, that our company should be welcomed with open arms, together with all foreign investments, in the new country. This message was [also] conveyed to me [...] personally and separately by Nawabzada Liaquat Ali Khan, who was an old family friend and had been a colleague of my parents in the UP Assembly. I was determined to do what I could in this respect.'† His wife and daughter joined him five months later in December 1947. Their family went on to establish deep roots in the new nation. They have produced three generations of women authors—Isha'at's wife, Jahanara, their daughter Muneeza (born in Lucknow in 1944, pre-Partition) and their granddaughter,

---

*'Tales of conflicts after the partition', *New Indian Express*, 5 April 2017. Retrieved on 21 June 2018. http://www.newindianexpress.com/cities/chennai/2017/feb/05/tales-of-conflicts-after-the-partition-1567311.html

†'Investing in Pakistan's Future', *Dawn*, 8 February 2011. Retrieved on 21 June 2018. https://www.dawn.com/news/604702/

noted writer, Kamila Shamsie.

The other brother, Ali, was already living in London at the time of Partition as part of the Indian High Commission. While he chose Pakistan, going on to become the Textiles Commissioner for the country, his wife, the eminent author, Attia Hossain, had a much harder time accepting the loss of their ancestral homeland. She had been born in Lucknow in 1913, studied at the Martiniere College and Isabella Thoburn College there, and also been married there in 1933. Her novels would later touch upon her pain of being separated from her parents, who stayed on in Uttar Pradesh, and from a centuries-old family legacy. Reminiscing about Lucknow, one of her characters in a short story says: '...everyone knew you and you knew everyone and there was no need to explain. You were part of the whole and the whole could not be but that you were a part of it. Without explanation. Just being.'* This longing for a home perhaps went on to her daughter, noted film-maker Shama Habibullah, who chose many decades later to return to live in India.

Enaith's fourth sibling, his sister, Tazeen was already living in Karachi since 1944, and stayed there post-Partition.

In the beginning, there wasn't a clear sense of what Partition meant for such divided families. 'People thought it would be like a Union, and that people would go back and forth,' muses Saif. In the early years, it was like that. All of Inam's grandchildren from Pakistan spent their summer vacations in their ancestral home in Lucknow. However, over time, the

---

* Rakshanda Jalil, 'A part of the whole', *The Hindu*, 2 March 2013. Retrieved on 21 June 2018. http://www.thehindu.com/books/books-reviews/a-part-of-the-whole/article4468920.ece

borders solidified. 'We completely lost touch with that side of the family. Communication between India and Pakistan is not that easy. That side of the family also did very well, but we are not really in touch,' says Saif.

A Delhi Staple

Kasturi Lal Wadhwa

**Born: 1930s in Rawalpindi, undivided Punjab
(now in Punjab, Pakistan)**

Kasturi Lal Wadhwa only studied till class six or seven because of the Partition; however, that did not stop him from growing a small kiosk into a restaurant that would be described by The New York Times in 1982 as having 'the best butter chicken tasted by civil servants and foreigners alike'. Today Pindi is ranked in the top 1 per cent of Delhi's restaurants. Kasturi Lal passed away in January 2010, so his story is told by his son Vinod Wadhwa.

'When my father came from Pakistan after Partition, he started by selling chana and kulcha in front of Baroda House. It was years later when the New Delhi Municipal Commission built Pandara market, that he was allotted a space here. He was the one of the first allottees, and so he had a significant role in building this market to what it is today, step after step, then another, then a bigger one, till it got to what you see now.' The Pandara Road market in central Delhi has changed from dhaba-style eateries to air-conditioned restaurants—but the flavour of the food remains unchanged, a touch of undivided India.

Kasturi Lal was around twelve years old when he came from Rawalpindi in 1948 with his parents and siblings. The family had travelled by bus and train from across the newly demarcated border. They had not managed to bring anything with them when they arrived in Delhi, so their economic situation was dire. They moved into a refugee camp in Jhandewalan, Karol Bagh, in New Delhi.

The young Kasturi Lal felt the full weight of economic responsibility. Though his father, Shivram Wadhwa, was trying to restart the masala business he had left behind in Rawalpindi, Kasturi Lal too felt that he needed to contribute to the family's welfare. He was conscious of the fact that he was the oldest of eight siblings, who needed to be fed and looked after.

He had only studied till class six at that point, but further studies were out of the question now given their financial circumstances. Kasturi Lal had already started helping his relations with their businesses in Rawalpindi. Now he knew that he would need to start working full-time.

The extended family spread to various parts of India—

some going to Kanpur and Lucknow to try find economic stability.

Kasturi Lal's future wife, Rajrani, too left behind a comfortable life in Jhelum in undivided Punjab. Rajrani's father (Vinod's nana or maternal grandfather) used to own a general store and had gained some influence and local standing in his community. He had, therefore, believed that they could stay behind in Pakistan. This proved to be a fatal decision. He was killed in the violence that shook Jhelum; his wife saw him being killed before her eyes. She believed that he was targeted because of his wealth. She succeeded to make it across with her daughter and two sons. She had managed to hide a little bit of gold and bring it with her, but other than that they had nothing. 'They really struggled in life in the beginning,' says Vinod. But his nani could not let herself look back because of her three young children. She somehow found a place to stay in Bhogal in New Delhi, and then moved nearby to a house in Jungpura. 'She was a very strong lady,' remembers Vinod. 'She raised three children all by herself.'

Kasturi Lal's father, Shivram, meanwhile started again to make the chana masala, chaat masala and other spices that had been the family business before. These had a distinctive flavour, and in fact, even till date form the 'secret sauce' behind the Pindi restaurant's dishes. Kasturi Lal's mother, Rampyaari, was a housewife and focussed on looking after the large family. Meanwhile, Kasturi Lal started selling chana and kulcha near India Gate. His father's spices gave a zesty taste to the food, so business grew quickly.

In 1959, the Wadhwa family's fortunes started turning for the better. They were allotted a shop in the newly built Pandara Market in Delhi. As Shivram was occupied with the spice business, it fell on the young Kasturi Lal to build this business.

He decided to start a small eatery and to name it in memory of the home they had left behind—'Pindi' (this is the colloquial moniker for Rawalpindi even today). By then the family had managed to move into a small place in West Patel Nagar, and Kasturi Lal had gotten married.

'When we were first allotted this place, it was just a small kiosk. People would sit outside. There was no indoor seating. First, we started with putting a fan, then a cooler, and then much later, an air conditioner—that is life, step by step.' The family have a 99-year lease on the shop from the NDMC. Vinod guesses that the rent was hardly one rupee a month in the early days, now it is still only ₹3,000. 'One wouldn't be able to get a place like this today for less than some lakhs. The government really helped us by allotting us this shop.'

The market then had only vegetable and grocery shops, so it fell to the young Kasturi Lal to also start building a customer base. In 1959, the competing Gulati's opened in the market—but rather than viewing it as a threat, Kasturi Lal saw it as a boon to build footfall in the market. Later, he also helped the neighbouring Krishna sweetshop establish itself.

Slowly Kasturi Lal's siblings started coming of age and helping the family. One started Pindi Cloth House in Connaught Place (which still exists today), another became a doctor. From what Vinod remembers, the family was allotted a plot in Kalkaji for ₹11,000 in 1967.

In the Pandara Road restaurant, Kasturi Lal worked day and night to establish the family again. 'I saw him work from nine in the morning till two at night every day. He would work so much that he didn't know which class I was in at school, he just felt that he needed to re-establish the family income.

'Once upon a time, it was very difficult to run a profitable business in this market, because it is inside the colony. But our parents worked very hard. Today, we are enjoying the fruits of their labour. We don't have problems only because of them.' When the restaurant began it could seat only about 10 people; it took four decades of toil to convert it to a hundred-seater.

Kasturi Lal was never able to go back to his hometown, Rawalpindi, which gave his restaurant its name. 'He wanted to go back and see everything again but he couldn't as he didn't have a passport or visa.' However, a branch of the family had stayed back in Pakistan at Partition as they had felt that they would economically be better off there, so when they visit, they carry tales of Rawalpindi, as do other tourists from Pakistan who keep coming for the famous food at Pindi. Through them, the family has heard stories about their town and the changes there. They know, for example, that their house is still standing, though of course occupied by others now. Traces of Kasturi Lal's old life remained even in Delhi: 'He read and wrote only in Urdu. He read Urdu newspapers, signed in Urdu and kept his account books also in Urdu.'

Kasturi Lal died in his eighties on 25 January 2010. His legacy, however, lives on.

The restaurant he grew from a little roadside stand sees a lot of happy repeat customers. 'Last week one person who ate at the restaurant said, "I am living abroad; after 40 years I am eating at this restaurant again."' While some things have of course changed with time—like earlier, roti would be given free with the food items—others have stayed the same, most particularly the taste of its core dishes, based on their family recipes. Today, Pindi is ranked in the top 120 out of more than 12,000 restaurants in Delhi. This puts it in the top 1 per cent in the nation's food loving capital—no mean feat. Even its younger Bangalore outlet is rated in the top 10 per cent restaurants in that city.

Though Vinod was born nine years after the Partition, he can imagine the pain that the riots caused his family, for he saw the same inferno erupt in 1984. 'I saw a lot of things in 1984: one of my good Sikh friends was killed. He and I were coming back after playing together in Saharanpur, and the situation was getting bad, so I told him to stay here with us, but he insisted on returning to his house in Palam as his brother was home on leave from the air force. They both were burnt alive—the mob threw burning tyres on them. Both the brothers died on the spot. In the house right in front of ours in Kalkaji, they killed a Sikh man. After that, the family sold off the flat for just 3 lakh and went away. That property could have fetched so much more, but they took whatever they could get and fled.' The 1984 riots were a painful reminder for the Wadhwa family of all that they had lost in 1947–48.

I Have Always Felt Like a Refugee.
I Still Do

Krishen Khanna

Born: 1925 in Lyallpur, undivided Punjab
(now Faisalabad, Pakistan)

Krishen Khanna is a leading artist in India. He has received the Lalit Kala Ratna from the President of India (2004), the Padma Shri (1990) and the Padma Bhushan (2011). His works are collector's items; for example, a single canvas was sold at Christie's Auction in 2008 for $1,81,000.

Krishen Khanna may have become a painter even if he hadn't experienced the horrors of Partition. However, in a strange way, Partition led him straight into the arms of his true calling. 'It is very strange that something as horrible as Partition became an opening for me,' he says. 'But, personally, that is how I got to Bombay, got to know all these eminent artists, got into painting. It is very odd, but it happened that way.'

Khanna was born in Lyallpur (now Faisalabad in Pakistan) in 1925. His father, K.C. Khanna, came from a humble background. As a young child, his father had lost his right arm in a freak accident while trying to rescue his sister who was caught in a whirlwind. As a result, his education was interrupted. However, he persevered. He began studying secretly at night, then enrolled in the local village school, till eventually he went on to do a PhD in London. By the time Krishen Khanna was born, his father was well established as a professor of History.

Khanna's formative years were spent in Lahore at the Cathedral School, while his father taught at the Government College. When Khanna was about 11 years old, the family moved to Multan as his father was posted as the Divisional Inspector of Schools there. After about a year and a half there, Khanna's father arranged for him to take an exam and interview for pursuing his education in England.

At the age of 12–13, Khanna went to Imperial Service College in Windsor on a scholarship. He made the journey alone, and for four years—from 1938–1942—did not see his family at all. However, the young boy found his feet in the new country, throwing himself into sports. He became captain of the fencing team, in addition to playing rugby and cricket.

But World War II brought dramatic changes—Khanna's school headmaster told him in 1942 that he would have to return to India by the next available ship as there might not be another opportunity. In the three-month-long journey from Liverpool to Bombay (now Mumbai), Khanna unfortunately witnessed his cabin mate passing away from a long affliction with tuberculosis.

Coming back at the age of 17, Khanna had to again throw himself into a different education system for his intermediate levels, and in particular, had to pick up Persian in less than eight months. But again, he did well, and graduated from Emerson College in Multan. Soon afterwards, his father was transferred to Lahore, and Khanna joined the Government College in Lahore for a BA in English. He also started to take evening classes at the Mayo College of Art in Lahore.

At graduation, Khanna told his father that he would like to teach poetry, but his father wanted him to join a bank. As a compromise, Khanna started working for a printing press in Lahore. He recalls days and days of standing in the intense summer sun of Lahore, bare chested, poring over photographs for blocks and plates.

Most of Khanna's workmen colleagues at the printing press were Muslim, and so were his friends. The idea of Partition, therefore, seemed preposterous to them even in 1946. 'There were Muslims, there were Hindus, and there was such amity I cannot tell you. When the disasters started, it was completely incomprehensible.'

Khanna, then 22 years old, remembers Lahore being in flames that summer of 1947. 'You could see it from where we were—flames going up, houses being burnt. *Allah hu Akbar* on one side and the other side *Har Har Mahadev* going on.' One

I Have Always Felt Like a Refugee

day, while his brother was playing cricket, the ball went out on the road. Though it was curfew hour, his brother ran out to pick it up but halted when he saw a military truck. 'This officer got down from the truck, and said you are very lucky you stopped when we asked you to, otherwise we would have shot you if you hadn't.'

It was in fact never certain whether the family would leave Pakistan. One day, as his father was wrapping up work, he told the peon, Ghulam Ali, who was still cleaning the place to also head home. However, Ghulam Ali, perhaps by some instinct, sensing danger, didn't leave and instead locked himself in the bathroom that night to try and learn more about the situation afoot. That night, Ali overheard people talking about unleashing mob violence the following day. 'The next morning when my father came, Ghulam Ali was there cleaning the room, and without looking at my father in the face, he said, "*Sahib, aap chale jaayein, maamla garam hone waala hai, log aane waale hain*" (Sir you should go away, things will get ugly, people are coming). My father understood what he was saying, and believe me, if he hadn't, then I wouldn't have been here. We packed and left the next morning with as much as we could carry. Just like that.'

Khanna's Partition journey was relatively safe as they drove to Simla in their own car without incident. The main challenge in the early days was that everything had been left behind; they had only been able to bring the bare essentials. Still, they were lucky that his father held a government job.

Khanna had taken a week's leave from the printing press at the time of Partition, thinking he would go back soon, but he never could. Punjab was in turmoil. Khanna and his family settled down temporarily at Tara Devi near Simla. His father was the head of the Punjab Boy Scouts: 'There was a Scouts outfit there with places to stay, so we were lodged there,' Khanna recalls.

Khanna's father would try to pay forward the kindness shown to him by the peon in Lahore. At Tara Devi, one day, when the family was having a meal, a senior person helping with refugee operations in Punjab—Sardar Hardayal Singh—came in agitated. The staff had earlier been a mix of Hindus, Muslims and Sikhs, but with the rising violence, the Muslims had all fled—only one person, called Shuja, was still there. Khanna's father had so far been hiding Shuja in his own house. Singh told Khanna's father that a telegram had come from Shuja's family, *'Kahaan hai beta, tu kahaan hai?'* (Where are you son, where are you?) it had pleadingly asked. Khanna recalls, 'In those days the railway station in Simla was also acting as a post office and also as a means for dissemination of information for everybody. So when this telegram came… people became aware that there is a Muslim around in this place.' Sardar Hardayal Singh was worried that a mob might form and target Shuja.

Khanna recalls that his father had a quick answer for the situation. 'Send the family a telegram back saying that Shuja has left for Lahore,' he remembers his father saying.

'I don't know the address of the family!' Singh replied.

'That doesn't matter, send it to any address.' The idea was not that that telegram would reach and assuage the family's feelings in Lahore, his father explained, but that in the local population the word would spread that Shuja has gone back, and so they would not hunt him down.

The ruse worked. The very next morning they helped Shuja escape: 'Shuja was put on an early morning truck loaded with timber…with wood and logs all over him covering him up, so that nobody would know that there is a person inside it. He was safely taken away to Simla and lodged in a refugee camp there,' Khanna remembers.

Khanna himself would also come forward to help get Muslim refugees safely to the train stations. His father also told him to go help at the Ambala railway station because many of his colleagues were still on their way. Their wives had come ahead, and Khanna would try to help them find their husbands in the middle of that chaotic, brutal atmosphere. 'These poor women, young and old ladies, waited for their husbands to turn up and nobody arrived. I tried to give such assistance as I could give.'

'The atmosphere was just terrible. People just didn't know what to do. They were just waiting for fate to happen. Many trains didn't arrive and many arrived totally [butchered]. They were all killed. People were dead.' Khanna painted this scene of the refugees waiting for the train at the railway station, years later.

Khanna also had to figure out his own future in the newly divided India. 'I couldn't go back to my job in Lahore so I didn't know what was going to happen to me and my future,' he remembers. Fate was kind. Khanna had studied at the Imperial Service College in London, and though as a rule he never wore ties, coincidence would see him wearing the tie of his alma mater that day. 'This chap recognized the tie…and asked me if I was in Imperial Service College and I said, "Yes, I was". After a while he asked me if I wanted to join the bank.'

Though Khanna had no interest in banking, what mattered at that point was an income. 'At that stage anything that brought in money and could pay for a livelihood was acceptable, so

I said yes and went for a five-minute interview with the chairman of the bank.

I remember when I went there he asked me to come in and said, "What makes you think that you would be a good banker?"

I said, "Nothing at all, sir". I had no idea that I could be a good banker.

He said, "Why do you want to join the bank then?"

I meekly replied, "Perhaps you have heard that there has been a Partition in this country..."

"You want a job." He had understood.

"Yes sir, I want a job." I replied.

He said, "Alright, you will get a job."

So, I was shunted off to Bombay and I was at that bank for close to 14 years after that.'

In Mumbai, Khanna would meet the Progressive Artists' Group (PAG), and this would redirect his life. But that would come later. His immediate thought was on rebuilding.

'The shock of it is so much that it doesn't leave you time to think about things like painting,' Khanna says. 'Any kind of traumatic situation is bound to leave a scar, and sometimes it opens up. But to think that it will immediately result in creativity is a fallacy. We would like to think it's so, but it is never like that. In the beginning, it is just about survival.' When he moved to Mumbai it was not with the idea of painting, it was instead to stand on his own feet again and make an income after Partition wiped away so much.

However, it was in his spare time in Mumbai that Khanna started painting more. He had been in Delhi on the day Mahatma Gandhi was assassinated and remembers that on his way home, around Connaught Place 'there was one lamp

91

and lots of people underneath reading newspapers with anxiety written on their faces and gestures'. The picture stayed in his mind, and it was the first one he painted after he moved to Mumbai.

This picture—'News of Gandhiji's death'—would rapidly change his life.

Shankar Balwant Palsikar, a leading artist in Mumbai and later the head of the JJ School of Arts, saw this painting on Gandhi's death, and asked Khanna to allow him to place it in the Bombay Arts Society Exhibition. 'He took it. He put it in the exhibition. It was a big exhibition, it was not the annual exhibition but a diamond jubilee or one of these,' Khanna recalls. The painting had pride of place, right in the center surrounded by the works of other famous artists, like M.F. Husain and S.H. Raza—artists who would soon go on to become Khanna's close friends. It was 1949. (That work would change many hands over the years; in 2005, it was placed on auction at Sotheby's for an expected price of $35,000–$45,000.)

'Soon, I was inducted into the Progressive Artists' Group by Husain,' remembers Khanna.

The PAG, formed in 1947, consisted of artists like M.F. Husain, F.N. Souza and S.H. Raza who wanted to develop a more modern, avant-garde style in India. Mumbai itself was a chaotic carnival of celebrities such as Raj Kapoor, Dev Anand and Zohra Sehgal, many of whom had their own stories of hard work and struggle. This group would encourage Khanna to continue painting.

From there onwards, there was no looking back. Six years later, in 1955, Khanna would host his first solo exhibition at

USIS*, Chennai. In 1957 (and again in 1961), he would take part in a group show at the Tokyo Biennale and in 1960 at the Sao Paolo Biennale.

It was another six years after that, in 1961, that Khanna would finally quit banking, after 14 years of service at Grindlays Bank. He doesn't, however, regret his time there though; he was happy, he notes. That time also taught him discipline that has served him well in his life as an artist.

Financial constraints had always stopped him from quitting before. When he had saved up ₹25,000 by 1961, and no longer felt he could balance the two professions of banking and art, he decided to quit. He recalls his friends from PAG celebrating with him that evening. Bal Chhabda (another artist in the PAG) pulled off Khanna's tie, saying he wouldn't need it anymore, and a celebration was held that evening with Chhabda, M.F. Husain and V.S. Gaitonde at The Coronation Durbar restaurant.

Khanna soon started receiving a monthly stipend of ₹500 from the Kumar Art Gallery in Delhi. He recalls the period as being one with a lot of hard work.

Soon after, Khanna became the first Indian to be awarded the Rockefeller Fellowship in 1962. He then became Artist in Residence at the American University in Washington in 1963–64. In 1965, he won a fellowship from the Council for Economic and Cultural Affairs, New York. Numerous international shows followed, including the Venice Biennale 1962, the Festival of India in the then USSR and in Japan in 1987 and 1988, respectively. Khanna also held several important positions in major cultural bodies in India, like the Lalit Kala Akademi

---

*United States Information Service, Consulate General of the United States, Chennai

and the National Gallery of Modern Art. He was awarded the Padma Shri in 1990, the Lalit Kala Ratna in 2004, and the Padma Bhushan in 2011.

But the turmoil and trauma of Partition never fully left Khanna despite his later successes. The memories stayed with him and have come out in his paintings at various points in his career. 'What happens is you carry images within you. If you are an artist, or even if you are not, you tend to carry images within you. It is those images which ultimately fructify. They materialize into work and this is what happened with me,' he says. 'When my father sent me [to the Ambala railway station] to receive people coming down from Lahore, I saw people sitting anywhere. They were anxious, bitterly anxious. There was a noticeboard there that said: "Refugee train 16 hours late". I painted that.'

94

He has not finished with the Partition series, says Khanna. And he doesn't want to sell these paintings. Today's generation doesn't understand Partition, he feels; they don't know Pakistan, they've never lived there. But he has and he knows what that separation means.

'You grew up with people, you spoke a language which was the same as them and all the teasing was done with them, you know. All that's disappeared. I have a lot of friends and people I know now, but the friendships don't have the kind of depth as it had with my childhood friends.'

He deeply feels the loss of a way of life left behind. 'I have always felt like a refugee. I still do. I still do.'

A Relationship of Loss Developed
Between Us

Kuldip Nayar

Born: 14 August 1923 in Sialkot, undivided Punjab
(now in Pakistan)

*Kuldip Nayar is an eminent journalist, a former Member of
Parliament in the Rajya Sabha, and a former High Commissioner
of India to the United Kingdom. Over forty years ago, he started
a midnight candlelight vigil at the Wagah border on the night
between 14 and 15 August.*

'I used to stay in Sialkot city with my family. My father was a renowned medical practitioner so we were a well-to-do prosperous family. We had property, servants, cars and everything else,' recalls eminent journalist, Kuldip Nayar.

He remembers the city as having a composite, syncretic culture. Their own family practised a mix of Sikhism, Hinduism and Sufism. His mother was a practising Sikh, who attended the gurdwara regularly, and had her children's names selected from the Guru Granth Sahib by a preacher as per Sikh customs. Hindu festivals like Diwali and Lakshmi Puja were equally celebrated in the house, and Kuldip's grandmother would regularly call the pandit to read their palms. Additionally, as in the family courtyard there was the grave of a Pir (a Sufi saint), the family would pray there every Thursday.

'All my friends were Muslims,' recalls Kuldip. 'We would go to each other's houses, celebrate Eid and Diwali together. One time, my friend, Shafquat told me, "You are my true friend, get a crescent and stars tattoo on your arm." So, I did. It was not considered a big deal.' But as the demand for Pakistan became clearer after the Lahore Resolution of 1940 (a meeting he had witnessed), Kuldip did feel that some rifts had begun to appear. This very tattoo would almost lead him to be lynched in 1947.

'Still, when the rumours about Partition began to spread in 1947, we decided that either way we were going to stay on in Sialkot. We used to reason that just like there would be a lot of Muslims who would stay on in India after Partition, a lot of Hindus would also stay on in Pakistan. In the Partition formulae, there was no mention of migration of population... Leaders used to refute that it would happen.'

Kuldip's family wealth was invested in Pakistan. 'Just a few months before Independence my father had used a lot of his savings to build a new house, dispensary and shop—all that property was of course not movable.' Therefore, the economic rationale to stay in Pakistan was also large. Kuldip's father at that time was past 60—moving to a new city to start his medical practice again seemed unthinkable.

Soon after the Partition, when the riots started and the mobs started burning homes and shops, the family realized they might need to leave Sialkot just till things calmed down again.

The family was still debating their plans, when on 12 September, an army officer who had been transferred to India came to their home, before leaving. 'He said "Doctor Saheb, you've been of great help to us in the past. We're now leaving, can we do anything for you?" My father pointed to me and my two brothers and said, "Take these three to Hindustan". The Brigadier looked very embarrassed and said that it would not be possible to fit three in the jeep, but he could take one with a handbag. So, my brothers and I started arguing, saying "you go, you go". Then, we took out a chit in a lottery type system and my name came out. I was the unwilling one who was sent ahead. I felt very scared that night about the future. The following morning, I took a small bag with two changes of clothes and left. I was so worried about my family and whether and when I would see them again.'

Kuldip was not expecting the devastation he saw on route. 'When we reached the main road—Grand Trunk road—I saw thousands and thousands of people. It was like all of humanity had come out on the streets. They looked devastated, their clothes were tattered, so many were injured... it was harrowing.

'At one point, when the jeep had stopped because of the crowd, an elderly sardar (Sikh) pushed a small infant towards me through the window. He said, "This is my pota (grandson), and out of our family of 40 people, he's the only one left. Take him to Hindustan with you." I was so flustered, I didn't know what to do. I said "I'm still studying right now, how can I take him?" He replied, "I'll find you, just become his guardian for now." I said, "This won't be possible, I can't take so much responsibility." But even now, I remember his face, a helpless man, saying "take this child". I've never been able to get over this incident, it still haunts me, there is a lot of guilt somewhere.

'All along the way, we saw village after village had been annihilated. We could see fires burning in the distance, and corpses and empty suitcases along the road.'

Just outside Lahore, the convoy was stopped. Kuldip and the officer's family feared an attack. Rumours were spreading that there had been an attack on Muslims in Amritsar, and so a mob from Lahore was waiting nearby to take revenge. The fears fortunately proved unfounded, and slowly the jeep made its way to the makeshift border.

'After arriving in Amritsar, I took the train to Delhi. I didn't buy a ticket because I had only ₹120 with me from home, and I wanted to save it for the coming days. Even though I had a Law degree, I wasn't sure if I would be able to start a practice in Delhi.'

On the way, the atmosphere in the second-class train compartment was charged. People were angry and grieving for their losses. The tattoo of the star and crescent was visible on Kuldip's right arm; a rippled murmur started that he was a Muslim. He was pulled out of the compartment at Ludhiana, and soon was surrounded by a mob of angry people. Some Sikhs with spears and swords loomed over him. He told them he was Hindu, but they did not believe him. In India, where circumcision is practised by Muslims but not by Hindus or Sikhs, Kuldip was saved this humiliation of proving his religion by the sudden appearance of an acquaintance from Sialkot who shouted out to the crowd that he was Doctor Saheb's son. The crowd slowly dispersed, and a very shaken Kuldip somehow made his way to Delhi. He had narrowly escaped humiliation and possibly death.

When he arrived in Delhi on 15 September, Kuldip went to stay with his aunt whose husband had a government job in Delhi. 'One night, I heard my aunt and uncle talking in the other room: "These refugees have come and they will make us refugees too—where will he go and how?" And then I decided that I have to think about something and find my own feet.

'One day, by coincidence I met a man near Daryaganj and I told him I was looking for work. When he learnt that I could speak Persian and Urdu, he suggested the name of a newspaper that was looking for people since their staff had left for Pakistan. The newspaper's name was *Anjam*. Anjam means "the end". So I always joke that *sahafat ka agaz maine anjam se shuru kiya*, that is, I started journalism from the end.

'When I reached the office, Yasin, the owner gave me something to translate as a test. And then, on the spot, he told me to sit on the desk and gave me a job. He said, "We will give you ₹100 per month."' Though Kuldip had intended to be a lawyer in Sialkot and had earned his LLB degree, with Partition's intervention, Kuldip's journalistic career had started instead.

Meanwhile, his parents were still in Sialkot. Around end October, they too finally realized that they would need to leave. 'Whenever they wanted to leave, my father's patients and friends would say "Doctor Saheb, we won't let you go

Who will look after our children's health?" But, not everyone felt that way. Others, even some who had been family friends, said, "Doctor Saheb, it would be great if you could stay, but it's our policy that we should not let Hindus and Sikhs stay. If you want to stay, you will have to convert." Then the thought of staying vanished.

'Finally, one day they got on the train to leave. Then some young boys recognized him and said, "Doctor Saheb, you're going in this train? We won't let you go in this gaadi [train]." My parents kept insisting that they needed to leave, but these boys insisted, "No, not in this gaadi. Tomorrow, we'll take you" and dropped them back to their house. The boys came back the next day, and said, that they had known the train the previous day was going to be derailed, so that was why they didn't let them go. They had checked and been assured that this one will go safely, so they dropped my parents to the station.'

His parents still believed, like so many others, that they would go back. 'I remember my mother told me that when she had set off she was wearing an expensive Shahtoosh shawl, but then she thought why spoil this in the journey and left it at home, and instead wore a Kullu shawl which is cheaper. She obviously thought she would come back to her things later. She also says as she put the lock on the house, she had a fleeting thought, that may be this was the last time she would ever return to that house. But she didn't give any weight to that thought. Everyone thought that there's "a bit of a problem, when it gets settled, we will go back to our homes in just a little bit of time". We never thought it was permanent, finished, and that we have to start over. We later realized that there was no question of going back.'

The small bag with all of the jewellery and cash that his

parents had brought with them was stolen on the way. So his parents found themselves, at age 60, having to rebuild their lives. They settled in Jalandhar.

Kuldip started to establish himself in the journalistic world. Soon, he got a job with the United States Information Service; this enabled him to enrol for a Masters in Journalism in the United States. As his parents were still struggling to make ends meet in Jalandhar, Kuldip had to take on a few jobs to cover his own expenses.

When Kuldip came back to India in 1952, he struggled to get a job. He came close at both *The Times of India* and *The Hindu*, but neither worked out. He tried sending stories to various newspapers, but they came back rejected. He stayed without a job for almost a year.

Finally, the first article that was accepted went to three newspapers—it was related to Partition, and titled 'To Every Thinking Refugee'.

Soon afterwards, Kuldip managed to get a job at the Press Information Bureau, and a few years later, became information officer for two successive Home Ministers, Govind Ballabh Pant and then Lal Bahadur Shastri. There was no looking back after that. He would later become the editor of the Delhi edition of *The Statesman* newspaper, the High Commissioner of India to the United Kingdom, and eventually, a Member of Parliament in the Rajya Sabha.

Decades later, this career would lead him back to Partition.

In 1971, he had a chance to interview Cyril Radcliffe who had drawn a line on a map—the border between India and Pakistan. 'I was writing a book, *Distant Neighbours*, on Partition. So I thought it necessary to meet the person who drew the line. I rang him up at his home in London, but he was reluctant to talk about that period and the region. He said it made him extremely unhappy. But I convinced him it's not a matter of sadness or happiness...it happened. He finally agreed.

'He lived on Oxford Street in a flat. The door opened, and it was Lord Radcliffe. At first, I thought it couldn't be him, because surely a Lord wouldn't be opening the door himself. But no one else came. He then proceeded to ask if I would have a cup of tea. I continued looking around here and there, expecting the real Radcliffe to emerge anytime soon. Once he had brought the tea, he said, "I feel sad talking about that time but ask me what you want to know."'

Radcliffe told Kuldip that initially Lahore was to come to India. 'He said, "At the time I drew the line initially, I gave Lahore to India. But, then I realized that Pakistan had no big city. Even in the East, I had given Calcutta to India, and Dhaka was not ready at that time, so I gave Lahore to Pakistan." I remarked that it was an extremely strange way to divide a nation. He said, "the problem of the division was that there were no maps available, no statistics or data. I had to draw a line on an ordinary map."'

Radcliffe had very little data to work with. 'He told me, "First, I thought I should use the Chenab as the border and then I felt the Ravi would be a better idea or maybe somewhere in between. But there was such little information." He was a sensitive man. He felt that what he had done had had repercussions, though he did not think he was responsible.'

Kuldip also met many of the other players involved in the Partition, from Mountbatten to Nehru to Patel to the members of the Boundary Commission, trying to piece together the puzzle of what exactly had transpired.

'I met Lord Mountbatten in Broadlands much after the

Partition. He didn't want to talk much about Partition. He felt that there was no other alternative. He said, "When I met Jinnah and Nehru and Patel, I came to the conclusion that the country staying united and in harmony would be difficult.'" But Kuldip could find no good answers on this quest to understand the event that shaped his circumstances so much by uprooting him and forcing him to a new place and life.

'A memory has stayed with me,' Kuldip says remembering his car journey from Sialkot to Amritsar in September 1947. 'When we reached the border in 1947, there was a sea of people going from Pakistan to India, and an opposite movement from India to Pakistan also. We stared at each other silently. They had also come after being looted, leaving behind all their friends, relatives, houses, property and everything and our story was also the same—we had left everything. But we kept looking at each other for quite some time—like a relationship of loss had developed—a relationship that both of us had become refugees, a relationship of sympathy, kinship.

'That is the reason why I have talked about soft borders for so long. For so many years now, maybe 20–30 years, I have been going to the border on the night between 14 and 15 August, and lighting candles there. Candles signify peace and are a light in the dark, so it was a message. It became a people's movement, with so many joining us. We sit for some time there, people on both sides on the border, and then after some time, we leave, knowing that we will meet again next year.'

The memories of Sialkot have stayed strong for Kuldip and come to him in strange moments. 'When I was in jail during the Emergency, one night I thought of the Pir whose grave was in the compound of our house in Sialkot. He came to me in my dream and told me that I would be released the following

Thursday. Strangely, Thursday was the day of the week when my mother and we, the children, would always light a candle at his grave. When Thursday arrived, I waited impatiently. The morning passed, then the evening, but nothing happened. The next day, early in the morning, the jailer woke me up and said that they had received papers for my unconditional release. I asked him when they had arrived, and he said, "Yesterday, Thursday, but we thought why should we send you in the night, we'll let you go you in the morning." You can call it coincidence perhaps… but when I told my mother, she insisted that I take a chaddar (offering) to Sialkot to put on the grave.

'I reached Sialkot and found my house, but I couldn't find the grave. It was now a few decades after the Partition. I asked a person there where the grave was. First he pointed to the larger public graveyard nearby. I said, "I know. I am from Sialkot. That graveyard is the regular one, but I used to live here, and there was a single grave here." This man then called the owner who said that when their shop had needed to expand, they had had the grave removed. I had taken the offering but the grave wasn't there.

'They said that I could see the house if I wanted. But I hesitated. I stood there feeling lost, thinking that a home is not made of walls and rooms, a home is made of neighbours and friends—here I didn't know anyone anymore. Everyone was new, the people sitting inside the house were new… It was their home now.

'I had waited almost 25–30 years to go back to our home in Sialkot, but I didn't linger there for even 30 minutes. There was nothing there that was known or familiar to me. A house or city is made of known people, friends, it's like a family of sorts. I just saw the house from the outside and left.'

Unsettled People Cannot Settle

Ajeet Cour

Born: 16 November 1934 in Lahore, undivided Punjab
(now in Punjab, Pakistan)

Ajeet Cour is an award-winning poet and novelist. She received India's highest literary honour, the Sahitya Akademi Award in 1985 for her autobiography, Khanabadosh. She has also been feted with the Padma Shri (2006), and the Punjabi Sahitya Sabha Award (1989), amongst others.

'When I was little, I was admitted to the Sacred Heart School run by Irish missionary nuns,' Ajeet Cour recalls of her childhood in Lahore. 'The nuns used to say, "There is a difference between K and C." According to them, K was masculine, while C was soft and feminine. So, I thought, "What is this masculine K doing in my name? It should be replaced by a C." And since then I started spelling my name as Cour.' This is a legacy of her childhood she has kept to this day instead of the more typical 'Kaur' in Sikh families.

When Cour was around nine years old, she was taken out of the convent school to be educated by Giani Kartar Singh Hitkari, the father of the eminent poet Amrita Pritam, to improve her Punjabi. It was during these months that she would be introduced to all the major Punjabi poets like Waris Shah, Peelu and Bulle Shah. 'During that time, my interest in Punjabi literature grew. I dreamt that even I would write poetry some day.'

Born in an affluent family of Lahore in 1934, Cour grew up in a large haveli on Chamberlain Road, where her father had a homeopathic clinic on the ground floor. Her nanaji* (maternal grandfather) owned a lot of land around Gujranwala (now in Pakistan) with fruit orchards, and Cour spent her vacations there.

However, despite the affluence, Cour's childhood was a lonely one. Brought up by a disciplinarian father who didn't believe girls should be educated, or even venture much out of the home, Cour retreated increasingly into an inner world.

---

*Bapu Ishwar Singh, who Cour called 'nanaji', was actually her grand-uncle. Singh had adopted Cour's mother as he had no children of his own.

Though she excelled in her studies, clearing a University level exam at age nine, her education was sporadic and intermittent, with her father periodically removing her from school for household chores or because she disobeyed his instructions.

The riots in 1946 and 1947 were a disruptive shock to Cour and her family. 'The atmosphere had been one of friendship as well as discrimination. You could not eat food cooked by Muslims, you could not drink water offered by Muslims. I still remember, at the stations, there were large drums kept separately with water meant for the Hindus and water meant for the Muslims. They were labelled as "Muslim Water", "Hindu Water". These differences did exist but these were not the kind that would make people start killing each other.

'My nanaji's closest friend was called Haji Saheb. Haji Saheb used to take him home secretly for dinner/lunch. Sometimes he would take me along too but he would say don't tell your nani that we ate at Haji Saheb's home.'

But things rapidly changed in 1947. 'From Rawalpindi, large groups of people fleeing the riots, the looting and killing, came to Lahore. My mother and I went to the camps to give people blankets, quilts and other items they needed and my father used to help people with medical ailments, giving them medicines. When we used to go to the camps we heard stories that were extremely frightening—"We killed the women of our families in order to ensure that their honour was protected", "My husband killed our daughters with his own hands with his sword", or "Our daughters and daughters-in-law jumped into wells to kill themselves so that they would not lose their honour". So all these people, who had lost everything, came to Lahore and stayed there and we would hear their stories and start crying. We didn't know that soon the same thing would happen to us.' At the time, early 1947, Partition was still an unbelievable idea to those in Lahore. 'All the leaders had said that anyway Partition was not going to happen. [Mahatma] Gandhi had said that "Partition would happen over my dead body", so we thought Partition would not happen.' And even in their moments of doubt, there seemed one surety: 'Lahore was the safest place because Lahore would stay in India—everyone believed this,' she remembers.

But by May 1947, the situation in Lahore was becoming dire. 'By May, fires from riots had become very frequent. All night, people would stand on the terrace and see that Shah Alami [a largely Hindu neighbourhood in Lahore] had been set ablaze, and Bhati Darwaza was burning. All night you could hear shouts of *Allah hu Akbar, Nara-e-Takbeer, Allah hu Akbar*, and people would come running and set houses on fire.'

One such night, standing on their terrace, they witnessed a particularly gruesome incident in front of their house that would force the family to consider leaving their home. 'A man came running through the darkness and there were around six others running behind him. There was a lane in front of our house and they entered that. The moment they turned into the lane we heard a loud shriek and the person who was running ahead collapsed. The rest ran away. We didn't know what exactly happened. We knew that since that man had dropped down, he had been stabbed. But the next morning we saw that his intestines had spilled out from his body. He was lying there and his intestines were lying next to him. On seeing that extremely scary scene, we decided to leave Lahore.'

Cour's father, Dr Makhan Singh, decided to send the entire family to Shimla for a month till the riots calmed down.

Even then, this was seen just as a very temporary move.

'Everyone said Partition isn't going to take place—it's just an uproar that is going to last a few days,' recalls Cour. 'Even until recently, my nani would say "rauliyan velay" or "jadon raulay paye san" [at the time of the tumult], because everyone considered it to be a temporary uproar.'

The family didn't take many personal or household items with them. 'We had a small iron trunk, in which we put the clothes for all four of us. Everyone was asked to keep two sets of clothes saying that it was enough for a month, and if need be, we could always buy more—we had the money. So we took one trunk and left our home. One small iron trunk.'

Cour's maternal aunt lived in Shimla and helped the family find a house to rent. Little did they know then that they would stay in Shimla till November 1947.

'The trouble in Lahore kept increasing and then the trains full of corpses started arriving—from that side to this side, and from this side to that side. The violence just kept increasing, and it reached such a level that we were unable to go back.' The family was in Shimla in August 1947, and it was here that they heard of the Partition of the country, and more devastatingly that Lahore would go to Pakistan. Cour recalls the radio announcements when they heard that bank accounts were being frozen. 'In one minute we became paupers. One minute we had lakhs and the next we had nothing.' With the loss of Lahore, the family had lost their home and the life they had known.

Cour's paternal grandparents were still in Lahore, and needed to be found and brought to safety. Makhan Singh decided to return to Lahore to bring them back. 'Everyone told him that going means assured death, but my father did not listen and left from Shimla.' It took Makhan Singh almost 12 days to travel the short distance from Shimla to Amritsar, and another week to find the means and permissions to travel the mere 30 miles from there to Lahore. When he reached, he soon learnt that their house had been taken over by refugees from Amritsar. His parents were at the camp. 'My grandfather and grandmother were found at the camp in a bad condition. They were crying, saying "we have abandoned our home and come here."' Makhan Singh reached out to his friend, Dr Muhammad Yusuf, for help in recovering the Guru Granth Sahib, the holy book of the Sikhs, from their house. Singh made his way back to Shimla with his parents and the Guru Granth Sahib. On the way there and back, Makhan Singh saw more evidence of the violence that overtook Punjab in those terrible months—trains with butchered bodies, corpses on the road and the misery of the refugee camps.

Slowly the rest of the extended family also arrived. The one person who was still missing was her maternal grandfather. 'We would go looking for him on all the trains from Gujranwala, and check with anyone from there if they knew of Bapu Ishwar Singh. We were told that he had set up langar at the station in Gujranwala and was feeding the refugees as they pass through the station. Though he faced the real threat of being killed, he said that while I am alive, I cannot let these people who have lost everything, go hungry. So, he remained in Gujranwala for almost four months with his langar after Partition.' Eventually, he too made it across safely.

Cour's family struggled for a few months to find their feet. They moved briefly to Jalandhar, but an outbreak of cholera forced the family to reconsider staying on. One day, 'Ranbir ji who owned the *Milap* newspaper came and told my father, "all your patients have reached Delhi and you are sitting here".

He got a truck and loaded the few things we had, utensils and everything, and we moved to Delhi.

'We had an acquaintance in Dev Nagar who gave us his house on rent. My father was allotted a clinic in Karol Bagh and he began his practice there.' Over a period of time, through the property claims process run by the Ministry of Rehabilitation to compensate refugees for the land they had left behind in Pakistan, the family was allotted a plot in Patel Nagar in Delhi. Makhan Singh's practice picked up again.

Cour resumed her education in Delhi. By mistake, she was registered as having completed the tenth standard. Through a scheme for refugee students run by the government, Cour was able to complete her BA when she was just 16 years old.

It was also around this time though that she got her break in writing. 'After coming to Delhi, I wrote a story that I read aloud at an inter-college seminar. And there, the editor of the magazine, *Naviyan Keemtan*, Professor Ram Singh, sent me a note saying he would like to publish it. In this manner my first story was published through luck and then I started writing more and more stories.' Cour went on to complete her MA degree at Camp College, an evening college set up especially by Punjab University for refugees. The building functioned as a school in the morning, and became a college in the evening. Cour would have preferred a degree in English Literature, but her father did not allow that because he found the class timings inappropriate, as the classes finished late in the evening. Thus, she enrolled in a degree in Economics, preferring that over the option of not enrolling at all.

Cour had completed her post-graduation by the time she was 18. But completing her education so quickly turned out to be a problem, reflects Cour. 'If I hadn't done that, if I had completed it slowly, I wouldn't have gotten married so early. At that time I didn't think that completing MA would be a cause of problems for me, but then the family started saying she's sitting idle at home, get her married.' Her marriage was an unhappy one.

Her husband would physically and emotionally abuse her, cutting the already short wings of her freedom even further. She found her own being entirely trampled under her husband's domineering personality. This dominance only got worse with the birth of her two daughters, as her husband would now use them as leverage to ensure Cour's subservience to him. He controlled everything she did and all her choices—her work plans, the clothes she bought for the children, the household expenses, her daily routine and movement, everything. Cour felt constantly observed and fearful. In the eight years she lived with him, he threw her out of the house an equal number of times.

Somehow within this diminishing, fearful status, Cour found the emotional courage to move into a working women's hostel with her two daughters to try and start building a new life, one which was not determined by either her father or her husband.

Until that moment, Cour had hidden her writing from her immediate family. Her father, and later her husband, both viewed it as a source of shame, a dishonour to the family name, rather than a source of pride. Yet, Cour had persisted from childhood through this time, sending articles secretly to magazines and publications. Now finally, she could openly embrace her writing.

But the worst of Cour's life had not yet come. Just as in 1947, the night between 14 and 15 August had shaped her family's life and trajectory, so did the same night in 1974 sear itself into Cour's being forever.

A call came late at night with the ill news that Cour's younger daughter, Candy, who was in France on a two-month scholarship, was in hospital for burn injuries.

Cour rushed to France but within days, Candy had succumbed to the third-degree burns that had taken over her entire physical frame. This moment of losing a child, and knowing her intense suffering before death, shaped Cour forever. In her autobiography, she notes that it was Candy's death that taught her how to live.

Her writing continued. In her stories, the pain of all her experiences—a disrupted childhood, a fearful youth, an unhappy marriage, trying to raise two children as a single mother, the misery of losing a child—found a voice.

In 1985, Cour won the Sahitya Akademi Award, India's highest literary honour, for her autobiography, *Khanabadosh*. In 2006, she received the Padma Shri.

Cour was the driving force between an initiative to bring together writers and poets from India, Pakistan and other South Asian countries as a means of promoting cultural connectivity; the Foundation of SAARC* Writers and Literature works under the SAARC banner to promote people-to-people dialogue.

Decades after Partition, Cour returned to Lahore for a conference, and went looking for her old home. Chamberlain Road, once an upmarket residential colony, was in shambles. 'It had potholes and was so unkempt and shabby that I could barely recognize it. I could hardly even recognize my own house. We kept going from one end of the street to the other. We

---

*South Asian Association for Regional Cooperation

finally identified the house with a lot of difficulty. The platform in front of the house had been covered and shops had been constructed there. The house itself had been broken up into 10 different parts, with many separations.' When Cour went inside, she had a rush of emotions. 'I felt that the souls of my nana–nani, dada–dadi, of my family, were buried in the walls of that house. I could see them all in the walls. I wrote a story on it—*Sheher Nahin Ghoga*—the way a seashell holds the sound of the sea, the same way a city holds the sounds of times past.'

In Cour's writings, she has tried to uncover these 'sounds of time past'. 'Unsettled people cannot settle,' she reflects. 'They only look for a place where they can feel safe.' It took Cour a long time to find her sanctuary; she built it herself.

A Hero's Journey

Brijmohan Lall Munjal

Born: 1 July 1923 in Kamalia, Lyallpur district, undivided
Punjab (now in Punjab, Pakistan)

*Brijmohan Lall Munjal founded Hero Group with his brothers
in 1956, which went on to become the largest manufacturer of
two-wheelers in the world. He is widely regarded as one of India's
pioneering entrepreneurs. He passed away in 2015. Santosh
Munjal, his wife and partner in his life's work, reflects on his
journey.*

Before his death in 2015, Brijmohan Lall Munjal had a net worth of over $3 billion. From the young 24-year old who saw the family shop go up in flames in the riots of 1947, it had been an impossibly long journey of rebuilding his life from scratch.

Brijmohan Lall Munjal was born in July 1923 in a village called Kamalia in Lyallpur district (now Faisalabad in Pakistan). He had three brothers—Dayanand, Satyanand and Omprakash; it was with them that he would start a cycle parts business in Amritsar in 1943–44, which would form the kernels of the global giant the Hero group is today.

But in 1947, as the brothers saw the burnt remains of the shop in which they had invested all their savings and effort, none of this was apparent. Instead, they could only see the piled-up losses of inventory and assets that were reduced to ashes. Their parents' wealth too had been left behind in their ancestral home of Kamalia, which with the drawing of the Radcliffe line had become suddenly a part of Pakistan.

The brothers had to start from scratch. They recall that there were nights they slept on platforms, on benches, in dharamshalas, with no savings to fall back on.*

This was a sudden end to a business that had seemed poised for rapid growth. In 1943–44, recognizing that World War II was creating a local market for bicycle parts (since imported parts were no longer available), the brothers had started trading of cycle components. They had moved to Amritsar, which along with Ludhiana, had become a major hub for the manufacture of these parts, and had divided up the work. One focussing on

---

Dada Papa ki Kahani, a family documentary shared by the Munjal family in September 2016.

supply, another on operations, and the third on sales, and so on. Brijmohan's role was business development, which he was good at. He got orders from places as far as Quetta (Balochistan, Pakistan), and often large orders, which rapidly expanded their business; at one point, getting a single bulk order of 2,500 parts. The business was taking off rapidly.*

But all this changed suddenly in March 1947, when the riots escalated in Lahore and Amritsar. Suddenly Amritsar, which was a major economic and trading centre, came to a deathly standstill because of riots. Corpses lined the streets, and fires blazed at nights. It was in one of these fires in mid-1947 that their shop was burned, and with it their growth plans.

As the brothers contemplated moving further east from Amritsar, thousands and thousands of weary refugees poured into Amritsar from west Punjab by foot and by train. They had witnessed killing and misery on their difficult journey. One of those trains brought the brothers' parents. Another, the woman that Brijmohan would eventually marry, Santosh.

At the time of Partition, Santosh's family was living in a village called Samundri in Lyallpur district. The family had stayed back even after Pakistan was created in August because her father did not think they would need to move: 'He would say: "So many rulers have come and gone in the past too, but everyone has lived together for so long—Hindus, Muslims, Sikhs. The government may have changed again, but that doesn't mean we can't stay." He felt that there was a lot of love amongst the people,' Santosh recalls.

But by September, the riots had gotten much worse.

Despite their initial resistance, the family was forced to

*Ibid.

make their way to Lyallpur town to a refugee camp for safety. 'We tried to arrange bullock carts to come to Lyallpur, but that did not work out. Somehow, we found a bus. We had to pay the driver a lot of money but we reached Lyallpur. The government had set up a camp there, so people took whatever little space they could find there. It was a difficult situation—there was only one stove and so many families had to share it.

'We did not bring anything. We left the house open. Even the doors were open. We knew we wouldn't go back and we also knew we couldn't carry many things with us. How much could we take and what would we take? So, everyone took one small suitcase. We couldn't bring more than that.'

At that time, there was a lot of violence against women, and a lot of abduction. Fearing for the safety of his daughters at the camp in Lyallpur, Santosh's father sent them further to Amritsar on a military truck. 'The army took care of our food and safety, and we felt safe with them. But we were worried about our parents and other relatives. Our fear concerned them. They were left behind.'

Santosh's eldest sister managed to register them for an evacuee property in Amritsar, and so the girls moved in. 'When my father and mother came across later, we all stayed in the same house. Other relatives, like my sister's mother-in-law and her elder sister-in-law, also joined us.'

All around them in Amritsar they could see the burnt down and abandoned houses. Every day the kaafilas of refugees would arrive from both east and west bearing tales of misery and horror.

'We stayed in Amritsar for many days. But then, we realized that we would need to leave Amritsar to find work. One of my uncles lived in Panipat and worked in a factory that made blankets, so we went to him. He put us up in the factory for a little while.'

Santosh's father was a doctor, as was her brother; they both started working again and the family tried to put the trauma of their difficult journey behind them to start life anew in a new city they did not know.

At that time, Santosh was already engaged to Brijmohan. Relatives had arranged their match in Lahore earlier, but amid the chaos of Partition, the wedding was delayed. Soon, however, in a simple ceremony, they would get married.

But in 1947, as Brijmohan stood with his brothers by the remains of their burnt shop in Amritsar, they were steeped in anxiety about their parents. 'Since their parents were still in Kamalia, everyone was very worried for their safety and how they would come across. They witnessed a lot of violence,' says Santosh. 'Kamalia was far from Lyallpur, and one had to travel from Lyallpur to Lahore and then Lahore to Amritsar.'

Decades later, Santosh returned with Brijmohan to Kamalia—the ancestral house looked exactly the same as Brijmohan remembered it. They were welcomed by the family living there. 'They asked us to come in and offered us water. They were very warm.' But in 1947, the situation had been dire. 'Everyone was just trying to get out alive... They faced immense difficulties,' says Santosh. The family's ancestral home and all their land in Kamalia was also lost during Partition.

Once their parents arrived, the Munjal family first tried to move to Agra. But they were unable to find adequate livelihood to support the entire extended family. The family then decided to move to Delhi.

Around this time, Brijmohan and Santosh got married. 'As many relatives who could come in the circumstances, came.

But it was a simple wedding. I don't remember much about whether anyone gave anything to me or not because nobody had anything in those days. They would have needed to have something to be able to gift it.'

The family opened a store near the Red Fort. But Brijmohan had larger ambitions. He decided to shift to Bombay with his wife in his quest for improving their economic circumstances.

But this was not to be. Fate was still putting the young entrepreneur through more trials. 'An incident happened where we had given a man a lot of money as advance payment, but he disappeared with all the funds.'

Brijmohan joined his brothers again in the cycle trading business in Ludhiana in 1951. It was here, after four long years of economic hardship and struggle, that he would begin to find his feet again.

He soon realized that the growth of their trading business was constrained not due to their sales but due to their supply chain—they were not able to take more orders, because they could not fulfil them. 'He brainstormed about what to do because it was proving difficult to sustain [the extended family] on the basis of the current business. Then sitting at the back of that shop he started making a cycle part himself.'

The nearly penniless dreamer made the bold decision that the family should set up their own parts-manufacturing factory. New factory licenses were being given by the Government of Punjab to kickstart the economy. Brijmohan managed to obtain one.

Hero Cycles was born in 1956. 'It started with one part, then two, then three and it eventually grew. Soon they took more space on rent and started making complete cycles,' recalls Santosh. From bicycle chains, to freewheels, to the hubs, the manufacturing business kept expanding till they were manufacturing complete bicycles.*

A visionary, Brijmohan, realized the importance of dreaming big and of the highest quality standards. Within a few years of starting Hero cycles, he was travelling to places like Germany to source world-class components and technology. The focus on efficiency and value led Hero to continue gain market share at the expense of existing manufacturers. By 1975, Hero had become the largest bicycle manufacturer in India. In 1986, the company was included in the Guinness Book of World Records for producing 18,500 cycles each day.

But fortunes would really take a different turn with their joint partnership with the Honda group in the 1980s. The Japanese company had put out an open call in a newspaper to find an Indian partner for a joint venture. Honda was impressed with the attention to detail, the supply chain systems and customer orientation at Hero. 'It was his ideas that they liked; the business itself was not that large at the time. Honda said that your way of working and ours is the same which is based on continuous effort.' The famous Hero Honda partnership was born. In time, the company went on to become the largest manufacturer of motorcycles in the world.

The journey is even more remarkable given the context in which Brijmohan built this global corporation. '[When] we got freedom, the country got divided with a lot of pain, trauma and problems. The actual economy started working only 1950 onwards, and that too with very limited resources, practically no resources at all. The availability of foreign exchange, technology, equipment and foreign technicians was very limited. We had

*Ibid.

to pass through all that,' stated Brijmohan in an interview in 2002.*

Brijmohan was awarded the Padma Bhushan by the Government of India in 2005 for his contribution to trade and industry, and many other awards like Entrepreneur of the Year in 2001 from Ernst & Young, and the Lifetime Achievement Awards from the All India Management Association, TERI and Ernst & Young in 2011, to name a few.

Santosh remembers that her husband 'always believed in thinking big, but he was also immensely disciplined in working on his dreams.'

Reflecting on his career, Brijmohan said in an interview in the early 2000s: 'If one puts in one's honest best, in a consistent, planned manner, and doesn't try to become rich overnight, you're bound to succeed. I also had an ambition once of becoming very rich very soon, but no, the process does not allow shortcuts. You have to proceed in a phased, planned manner.'†

The penniless dreamer had started a business from the embers of 1947 that went on to sell a staggering 5.5 million cycles in 2014.

*Speech by Brijmohan Lall Munjal in World EOY Country Highlights India, 2002; shared by the Munjal family.
†Speech by Brijmohan Lall Munjal at Ernst and Young awards, 2001; shared by the Munjal family.

My First Memory of Fear

Govind Nihalani

Born: 19 December 1940 in Karachi, Sindh
(now in Pakistan)

Govind Nihalani is one of the most celebrated film directors and cinematographers in India. He has won over six National Film Awards, and five Filmfare Awards. His TV series, Tamas, based on Bhisham Sahni's novel by the same name, is regarded as one of the pioneering examples of Partition filmography. A Tamil adaptation (produced by Kamal Haasan) of his film Droh Kaal was sent to the 68th Academy Awards as India's official entry in the Best Foreign Language Film category.

'I was born in 1940 on 19 December in Karachi. Our house used to be in the locality known as "Nayi Chali". We had a four-storey building, with many offices in the building, and our residence was on the top floor. Outside our building was an almond tree. I remember when the riots broke out, one evening, a person who had a shop under that tree, ran up to our house, and handed my father some money for safekeeping, and then he ran away,' recalls Govind Nihalani.

Govind grew up in a large joint family with many cousins. He remembers the months when suddenly their carefree play on the terrace became increasingly restricted. The young cousins had picked up the chants of Independence around them and would march around the terrace saying 'Hindustan Zindabad' or 'Inquilab Zindabad', with their home-made toy flags. But their parents worried that the sound of their childish squeals and games might carry down to the road outside, and Govind remembers his mother stopping their games around the time of Partition.

'One evening, we heard shouts from the street. They weren't very loud sounds, but they created a panic in the house. The doors and windows of the house were closed, and my mother, my aunt and other ladies of the house started whispering amongst themselves, trying to figure out if everyone in the family was safe at home or not. And then I heard *woh nahi aya, nahi woh bhi nahi aya* (he hasn't returned, no he hasn't returned either). That's when I came to know that there is something called "fasaad" (riots). That word struck me. There was something called a fasaad that was happening down there somewhere.

'After this, my father and my uncles covered the entire

balcony with gunny bags, so that nobody from outside could look in. Every evening, my father and my uncles peered through the gunny bags and kept watch on what was happening downstairs. There was a real fear that we were being watched. My first memory of fear is from this period—that something might happen to us.

'Soon after that, I came across another unfamiliar word, "curfew". "*Curfew lag gaya, curfew lag gaya*" (a curfew has been declared). Everything was silent. Even in the house people used to speak to each other in whispers. There was so much silence. And one afternoon, in the middle of that silence, I heard a man's scream. I rushed towards the terrace and I saw a man running, and suddenly, he was reeling on the ground with red blood oozing out of his back and he was screaming. My mother came running and pulled me away from the terrace immediately, so I must have seen that incident for only a few seconds, but those seconds stayed with me, like when you take a photograph. That incident became a defining visual, which I kept seeing. Even years later, when I was making *Tamas*, the incident became a very important visual of that period. It was my first sight of blood. I was on the fourth floor, so perhaps my memory is expanding that blob of blood on the back of that man, but I have never forgotten it, or the scream that I heard.'

The family found themselves slowly living in a state of siege. The women in the family started keeping red chilli powder with them to fend off an attack. The fact that the family was well-known and affluent increased the fear of an attack.

Finally, they decided to temporarily seek refuge in Rajasthan. Govind doesn't remember when exactly they left, but he remembers the flight. The family got nine tickets, divided into three flights. I was in the first batch with my mother. My

125

father stayed back because it was decided that the women and children were to be sent first. Much later, I was told that there was an attack on our building soon after we left. The mob was banging on the door of our house, but thankfully my father was able to call the police before they could break down the door. Our family was saved.'

The rest of the family also fled Karachi soon after. Though the initial idea had been to return after the riots calmed down, this became impossible as time went by, and they had to rebuild their lives in Rajasthan. The family was spared the misery of the refugee camps, as they had managed to bring enough money with them to rent a house. They started a grain wholesale business in Udaipur and began working towards building their own house in a new refugee township called Pratapnagar. The family had also brought with them some of their accounting books showing the rent they received from tenants in Karachi, and they used these to file a property claim with the rehabilitation ministry.

The new refugee colony was being established by the Government of Rajasthan to rehabilitate refugees coming from Pakistan; the government had allotted 625 bighas of land in total in the outskirts of Udaipur, in the villages of Sundarwas, Madri, Barda and Bedwas for the new township. Every morning my father and my uncles walked three miles to supervise the construction of the house, then back again on foot. There were no buses in that area.'

Govind had so far been home-schooled in Karachi, but now in Udaipur he started going to a regular school. After matriculation, as he decided what to do next, fate intervened. 'I was going through various options and was considering radio engineering or civil engineering, something where I could help my family. One day, I came across an ad in the paper for a course on cinematography. I wanted to pursue it, but initially my father said no. My aunt and uncle tried to persuade him. Finally, he agreed to consult the family guru. Our guru, Brahmanandji, examined my janampatri and he said it showed that I would work in a field that mixed machines and art, and that, since in cinematography the camera is mechanical and the work is art, I should go for the course. My father then agreed, so I enrolled in a course in Bangalore.'

In fact, looking back today, Govind points to a moment in his childhood in Karachi that perhaps laid the seeds for his fascination with films. He had grown up in a religious Vaishnavite family that didn't watch movies apart from those with a spiritual message. Thus, the first movie Govind saw was *Narsi Bhagat* based on the life of Gujarati poet-saint Narsinh Mehta. The film made a deep impression on the young Govind: 'In the scene, there was a young boy feeding pigeons. Then the camera zoomed in to focus on the pigeons while the song played. Then something happened, which in retrospect, I realize was the screen dissolving into another frame. And suddenly, there was another set of pigeons, and the camera slowly zoomed out, and in the frame, an older man wearing similar clothes to the boy was feeding the pigeons. All this happened as the song continued. And I remember the excitement I felt in my mind as I realized that the child had grown up. For me, that was a very magical moment.'

But when Govind completed his cinematography from Shree Jayachamarajendra Polytechnic (the present Government Film and Television Institute), he realized he had no connections in the industry. With a little research, he found out that the acclaimed cinematographer Venkatarama Pandit

Krishnamurthy (known in the industry as V.K. Murthy) was an alumnus of his institute. He decided to take a chance and go to Bombay to meet him.

Murthy was shooting for *Love in Tokyo* (1966) at that time and told Govind to join him on the sets just to observe. Murthy gave the young Govind his first break and took him on as an assistant. From *Baharon Ke Sapne* (1967) onwards, Govind assisted Murthy on most of his films.

Fate had even bigger plans. His friend Satyadev Dubey introduced him to Shyam Benegal. Benegal had just returned from the US and wanted to make his first feature film, *Ankur* (1974). He had written the film while in college and had been trying to find financing for the film for many years, but with no success because it was a serious film looking at a social issue of the feudal system in rural India. He was keen to cast a known actress like Waheeda Rahman, but after her refusal, he decided to give the opportunity to the then newcomer, Shabana Azmi. Govind could not have known when he signed the film as cinematographer that it would be the start of a long partnership with Benegal, or that the film would achieve such high critical acclaim. The film was runner-up at the National Film Awards for Best Feature Film (1975) and won both the Best Actor and Best Actress awards. It also made an international mark, with a nomination at the Berlin International Film Festival (1974) for the Golden Berlin Bear award.

Govind then proceeded to work with Benegal as a cinematographer on his forthcoming films, *Nishant*, *Manthan* and *Junoon*. Govind won the National Film Award and the Filmfare Award for cinematography for *Junoon*, thus firmly establishing him in the industry.

He had simultaneously started working as a Director on

his first feature film, *Aakrosh*. This was released in 1980 to critical acclaim. It won a National Film Award for best film, and six Filmfare awards in different categories.

Govind went on from there to make many more moving, powerful films, many on important social topics. One of these brought him back to Partition—*Tamas*.

'I was shooting for *Gandhi* in Delhi (Govind was an assistant director on the famous Richard Attenborough film) and one evening, I was just browsing idly in a bookshop, and the name of this book *Tamas* (Darkness) caught my eye. I had not heard of the author or the book before, but the blurb revealed that the book was on Partition. Because I was working on *Gandhi*, I was reading a lot of Partition stories as research, so I decided to buy this one too. The next few days were very hectic with shooting, and I didn't have time to read the book. About a week later, I got home early, so I opened the book to read. I read the first sentence *"Aale mein rakhe diye ne ek jhapki lee"* (the lamp placed in the niche flickered)—and I don't know what it was about that sentence, a very simple one, but it hooked me. I couldn't put the book down, I couldn't rest until I had completed it. I made an instant decision that this was a film I wanted to make.'

By a lucky chance, Govind found funding for the film as well. He was in the office of Lalit Bijlani discussing another project, when *Tamas* came up. Bijlani became one of the main backers of the film and helped raise the rest of the finances. Govind moved quickly—he dictated the script himself to an assistant, and had the set constructed within two weeks.

Making the film had many sensitivities and challenges. Since the costs of taking the entire team to Punjab were too prohibitive, Govind recreated an entire Punjabi town on the sets. In the movie, there is a scene set in a gurdwara, so he also decided to recreate a gurdwara on a stage in the sets. Like many Hindu families in Sindh, Govind grew up with a strong Sikh influence in the household. A Guru Granth Sahib was kept in the house, 'paath' was read regularly, and he remembers frequent trips to the gurdwara. 'This familiarity with a gurdwara helped me a lot when I was making *Tamas*, because Bhisham ji [the author] had an entire chapter set in a gurdwara. I could immediately visualize how to do the scene.' He still needed authentic extras. 'Luckily, at that time there were Sardars who were waiting to go to the Gulf as labour—they were mostly carpenters and manual labourers. We brought them in and shot in what they were already wearing for authenticity.'

The scene also needed a Guru Granth Sahib. 'I didn't want to get an original Guru Granth Sahib because there was so much chaos and mess around. We decided to just suggest the presence of a Guru Granth Sahib using an ordinary book covered in newspaper. Now, what happened was that when we called in the extras to explain the scene to them, the moment they stepped into the hall they took their shoes off and went and paid their respects to the Guru Granth Sahib. From then on, I informed everyone that even on the sets, no one was allowed to wear shoes in the area where the Guru Granth Sahib was kept, and no one would smoke a cigarette. The whole crew observed it. Whether the Guru Granth Sahib was real or not, for those who believe, that Guru Granth Sahib was real.'

But getting it released had its own set of challenges as protesters tried to block its release. 'The Shiv Sena protested, they wanted the film to be banned. I was put into police protection for eight weeks. The case went to the Supreme Court. We were very lucky to be defended by Soli Sorabjee.

We got the judgement in our favour.

'I remember when it started screening. I would be at home, and suddenly I could hear the 'Ho Rabba' soundtrack echo in my entire colony, in the seven–eight buildings around my house as all the televisions tuned in to this channel.'

The film went on to win many awards including Best Supporting Actress, Best Background Score and Best Feature Film on National Integration.

Nihalani reflected on his career. 'We started a movement of new cinema or parallel cinema as a reaction to mainstream cinema. They wanted stars, songs, dance. They wanted happy endings. We wanted to make a difference, we wanted to make change happen.' Nihalani has made many powerful films in his career spanning over six decades, but perhaps it was the unforgettable *Tamas*, drawing upon some forgotten memories of fear from his own childhood, that really shaped the way we remember Partition.

we remember.

We Get an Amnesia—
We Don't Want to Remember

Anjolie Ela Menon

Born: 17 July 1940 in Burnpur, Asansol, Bengal
(now in West Bengal)

*Anjolie Ela Menon is one of India's most acclaimed artists. She
has hosted over 50 solo exhibitions around the world. She was
awarded the Padma Shri by the Government of India and the
'Chevalier dans l'Ordre des Arts et des Lettres' (Knight of the Order
of Art and Letters) by the Government of France in recognition
of her work.*

'My father was a Lieutenant Colonel in the Army, and was in command of a hospital in Murree,' remembers Anjolie Ela Menon of the summer of 1947. 'Till the 21st or the 22nd of August, though Independence had taken place, everything seemed calm and quiet. We were not in a hurry to leave; we hadn't packed anything. In fact, there really had been no question of leaving Murree at that time because one had not foreseen such mayhem.'

But within a few days the situation changed completely. 'Around the 24th of August, my father went to meet one of his friends who was an older civilian doctor. There were rumours in the market that there is going to be trouble and that Hindus should leave, but this friend told my father that he was not leaving. He said that he'd been born and brought up in Murree and had practised there for the last 40 years, so the question of leaving did not arise.

'The next morning, we learnt that he had been found in a pool of his own blood. He had been murdered. That was the turning point for our family. My father decided to get the family out of Murree as quickly as possible.' The family drove down to the Army base at Rawalpindi in their jeep the same day. 'Most of our belongings were simply left behind. We had no time to take them.'

Anjolie was only seven years old at that time. 'I remember being made to lie down in the jeep because our vehicle was being fired upon. By the time, we got to the Army Mess, the situation had become very bad. Riots had started. People had started arriving wounded and dead from the Indian side of the border, and this was having an effect in Rawalpindi.'

Anjolie's father realized that he needed to evacuate the

133

family immediately. 'There was a military Dakota plane leaving Rawalpindi for Delhi, and my father managed to get a place for my mother, myself, my younger sister and one of our servants. I remember that we were sitting on the floor of the plane because there were no seats. There were a number of sacks and lots of soldiers. Only two families were on the plane—ours and another army doctor's family.' Because of the chaotic situation, the family had not been able to inform anybody in Delhi. 'In those days there were few telephones so we couldn't be in contact with anyone. Fortunately, my aunt was living in Sujan Singh Park, so we made our way there.'

But by this time, Delhi was itself in a tense state. 'Soon after we arrived, my aunt's dhobi walked into the house holding his intestines—his whole stomach had been slashed.' That disturbing image has stayed with Anjolie for over seven decades.

Thousands of Muslim families fearing attack had moved into camps set up across the city's monuments. Some sought temporary shelter there, others awaited evacuation to Pakistan. 'My aunt's servants were all Muslims. When the riots began and the trains started arriving full of dead bodies, Delhi also became unsafe. Homes were vulnerable to attack, so the servants all went to take refuge in Purana Qila where a huge camp had been set up,' she remembers.

The young Anjolie accompanied her family to Purana Qila, and the vivid memories of the camp have stayed with her. 'We went because one of my aunt's servants was having a baby. Some women surrounded her to deliver the baby, others held up a saree all around her for privacy. She had the baby under a tree. My aunt then brought the baby home because she realized that there was not enough food and water at the camp, and she felt the baby would not survive. I remember my mother and my aunt looking after this new born baby and feeding it with a bottle. It wasn't until two months later that the servants were able to return from Purana Qila.'

In the meanwhile, her father who was still in Rawalpindi, decided to return to Murree, in spite of the dangerous environment, to retrieve some of the family's precious belongings. He packed what he could in the jeep and made the journey again from Murree to Rawalpindi. 'He and another officer called Mahinder Batra and a doctor called S.N. Basu then joined a convoy of army trucks from Rawalpindi to Delhi.'

For weeks after that, the family had no news of him. 'They must have left around 29 August from Rawalpindi, but by mid-September they still hadn't reached and we had received no news. We waited and waited and we didn't know whether they were dead or alive.' With daily news of riots and killings through the radio and the papers, it was a harrowing month for the family. All around them they could see the situation spiralling out of control, and in the absence of any way to contact him, they feared the worst.

Her father did not reach till the end of September. 'My father, who was a surgeon, stopped on the way to operate on many people who had been wounded and left by the side of the road. He was stitching them up. Halfway through, they ran out of catgut, which is used for stitching, so they used ordinary thread. Then they ran out of anaesthetic, but there was a canteen truck with them, which had a lot of liquor on it, so they used that. They would pour liquor on the wound as a disinfectant, and make people drink it as an anaesthetic. It was mayhem. My father later wrote an account of what he saw—he said the river Jhelum ran red with blood. Kaafilas of thousands upon thousands of refugees were walking. Whatever help the army convoy could give, they did. They themselves didn't know how long it would take them to reach Delhi. They finally arrived a month later. My father was safe but completely shattered because of the hundreds of people he and Dr Basu had operated. The images of all the wounded and dead stayed with him.' But few people at that time would have thought about or paid attention to the mental and emotional trauma one undergoes when dealing with such grievous amounts of violence and death. Anjolie's father, like countless others, had to bear this burden alone.

Her father got another posting in the Indian Army, and the family followed him. Anjolie's rehabilitation to regular life was perhaps made easier by her father's profession. They shifted to a new town, and once again, the young girl threw herself into her school and hobbies.

Life would perhaps have continued as normal, but for the untimely death of her mother, Eunice, four years later, when Anjolie was 11 years old. Anjolie went to study at Lawrence School, Lovedale in the Nilgiri Hills, and this became a turning point in both her personal and professional life. It was here that she met her future husband, Admiral K. Raja Menon (they married in 1962, when Anjolie was 22 years old), and it was also here that she sold her first painting.

At Lovedale, Anjolie met art teacher Sushil Mukherjee, who became her guru, introducing her to the world of oil painting at the age of 12. Her natural talent could not be contained. At age 14, she sold her first painting to the then Vice Chancellor of the Aligarh Muslim University—and later President of India—Dr Zakir Hussain. There was no looking back after that.

After graduation, Anjolie went to the JJ School of Arts in Bombay (now Mumbai) briefly, but moved from there to Delhi to study at Miranda House. It was in Delhi that she met her second mentor, M.F. Husain. The eminent artist took her under his wing, giving her access to his studio. He even created the invitation card for her first solo exhibition, which was held when Anjolie was just 18 years old. The following year, aged 19, Anjolie won a scholarship in 1959 from the French government to study at the École des Beaux-Arts, Paris. These years were formative in further developing her unique talent as an artist.

Upon her return to India in 1962, Anjolie got married. The nomadic years of her childhood continued. If she had moved home over 15 times as a child due to her father's army career, she now shifted even more due to her husband's postings around the world. However, throughout this time, she kept painting and experimenting. Her natural talent and bold style captured the imagination of art collectors around the world.

She has held over 50 solo exhibitions, including a six-month solo show at the Museum of Asian Art in San Francisco. Her work is displayed in major museums and private collections globally, as well as in public spaces like the Delhi and Mumbai airport terminals.

In recognition of her contribution to art, she was awarded the 'Chevalier dans l'Ordre des Arts et des Lettres' by the French Government and the Padma Shri by the Government of India. She has also received a Lifetime Achievement Award from the Delhi Government.

A painting made by her in 1982 harks back to Partition. Titled, 'Mataji', the caption reads, 'She sits knitting in the sun, dreaming of Lahore in the days before Partition"*. Looking back over six decades of her career, Anjolie notes, 'It is surprising how little art came out on Partition. By the time I grew up and became a painter, I had repressed those memories. I think we get a sort of amnesia where we want to forget the horrible times and put them behind us. We don't want to remember.'

Perhaps it was not remembering (while never forgetting), which allowed Anjolie, her father, and countless others like them to reach beyond the pain to create new lives.

*Ritu Menon and Kamla Bhasin, *Borders & Boundaries: Women in India's Partition*, Kali for Women, 1998.

Milkha Singh, How Long Will You Keep on Crying?

Milkha Singh

Born: 20 November 1929* in Gobindpura, undivided Punjab
(now in Punjab, Pakistan)

Milkha Singh, also known as the Flying Sikh, is one of India's most decorated athletes, having broken numerous world records in the 1950s and 1960s. He was awarded the Padma Shri in 1959 for his achievements.

---

*There is some uncertainty about Milkha Singh's date of birth. He follows this date as this is the one he found in his school records in Pakistan.

'I have been running my entire life,' begins Milkha Singh.

His school was 10 kilometres from his village. 'We would go barefoot to school,' he recalls. 'The patches of sand used to boil, so, we would run for a couple of kilometres continuously, and only when we found a grass patch on the sand or some shade, we would stop there to cool our feet, and then again, we would start running.' The teachers were strict, and the fear of being beaten either by the teacher or by his father would ensure that Milkha and his friend would make the long journey each day, even though it involved perilously wading through two rivers when neither he nor his friend knew how to swim.

The man who went on to be known as the Flying Sikh, and who won the gold medal in numerous international athletic contests, was born in a small, remote village called Gobindpura, near Multan. It was a simple, agrarian life he recalls. 'We owned a little land.' Child mortality was high in those days, especially since they were far away from the nearest city. 'My mother gave birth to 15 children, but seven passed away very early from cholera and other diseases. So, before Partition, we eight survived—five brothers and three sisters.' He falters and stops.

After a pause, he starts, 'When Partition happened, we were living in a remote village so there was no newspaper, no radio, not a single news report. But those who travelled to city to buy oil or clothes or trading goods, they brought news back slowly. They said that the city people are saying that we would have to leave our village. But when we would ask—"Why do we need to leave?", no one knew anything.

'As village people, we used to think—we have our land, cows, sheep here, if we leave all these things, where will we go without our land and our cattle? And if we go, how will we survive?'

For an illiterate village man, he explains, Partition was an inexplicable concept. Why would anyone divide their country? His family and neighbours did not know or understand that Partition could or would happen. And, certainly, they could not understand how they could survive far away from the only world they had known, from the village that their ancestors had lived in.

'Our village elders decided that we would not move,' he recalls. 'We were two villages, the other about two kilometres away. We both united and decided that we won't leave.'

This decision was supported by the village Muslims, Milkha recalls. 'They used to say you are our brothers. We used to go to their weddings, they used to come to ours. We would go to their homes on festivals like Eid to congratulate them, and they would come to ours on Gurpurab to congratulate us. We shared a brotherhood with our Muslim neighbours.

'But things changed when Muslims arrived from other villages. They accused our neighbours of sheltering us. They incited them saying, "Your Muslim brothers are coming dead from there; the trains are coming with corpses. How can you spare them?" These outsiders gave us an ultimatum, "If you want to live here, change your religion, eat beef, cut your hair, only then can you stay". Our neighbours then were helpless.

'Soon, we heard that a mob is coming to kill us. The panchayat made a decision that the women of both the villages will take shelter in the gurdwara. And the menfolk would guard the outside.'

Another panchayat meeting was held to decide what to do. Even as the meeting was being held, a large group of around 5,000 Muslims had surrounded the village. After a prayer meeting at the gurdwara, the elders decided that they would not convert to Islam, despite the danger to their lives. 'We sent an interlocutor, Mota Singh, with our message.

'The mob was sitting some 50 yards from our village, and they had already started a fire. Mota Singh went to them to tell them that we had decided that neither would we convert, nor would we leave our village, but we were ready to fight till death. They shot him from behind as he was returning to us. He fell down from his horse and died on the spot. At that point, the war began. They attacked us with swords, we attacked them.

'I have watched everything happen in front of my eyes. My brother and sister, my parents, all of them were killed in front of my eyes. And my father's only words were "Milkha Singh run and get out of here, Milkha Singh run and get out of here, they will kill you too! Escape!" I ran.

'I ran into a nearby jungle, and from there running and hiding, I somehow reached the train. I concealed myself in the ladies' compartment, under the seat. I knew if I was caught I would immediately be killed,' he remembers. The mobs were everywhere, particularly at the stations, but Milkha somehow managed to reach Multan. He sent a message to his brother who was in the army about the massacre in their village.

His brother, with great difficulty, managed to take an army truck to the village. When he reached, there were just corpses spread everywhere. Someone's head was lying in one place, someone's body in another. Dogs and vultures were eating the dead.

'My brother was not able to identify my father, my mother, or my brothers and sisters.'

After two—three days, most of the corpses were in decay

and had been attacked by dogs and vultures, so few corpses could be identified or assembled. 'The whole village was stinking. My brother collected as many bodies he could find, put petrol on them, cremated them and then he came back.'

Milkha pauses. 'Very bad things have happened with us. Today people have only heard stories, they don't know how many people died in the Partition and that all the people who died were poor. None of the rich died there. The rich were already long gone via cars, buses, planes. But poor people, how and where could they go? Lakhs of poor people died.'

Eventually, Milkha made his way to safety in a convoy arranged by the army. He first made his way to Ferozepur by train, and then to Delhi.

'All the refugees landed at the Old Delhi railway station... When I reached, I was all alone. No one was with me,' remembers Milkha. 'But there was a register where you could write your name, where you are from, how many of your relatives have survived, how many have died, the names of any who have survived.

'I explained to them that I belonged to this village, that my whole village had been slaughtered, this happened, that happened. I explained everything. Then they used to make an announcement at the Delhi Railway Station for all the refugees who arrived there. Every day, there were announcements "so and so is here, so and so's relative so and so is here, come and meet him, come and see him". The announcement used to continue all day and night.'

It was a terrible condition, Milkha remembers. The hunger was overwhelming, with nothing to eat. 'No one had water to drink, no one had food to eat, no one had clothes to wear. One dead body was lying here, another dead body was lying there, and people were sleeping in between. And when someone would come with food, they would throw chapattis like they were being thrown to dogs. But we were so hungry, we would jump to get something to eat. Those who were able to grab something, were able to eat, the others just slept hungry.' There was no sanitation, so cholera also spread quickly.

'I cried a lot in those days at the railway station,' Milkha remembers. 'And I kept on crying. But how long can a person keep crying like this? One day, two days, four days, five days, seven days? I kept on crying, and then I said to myself "Milkha Singh, how long will you keep on crying?" So I decided to come out of the railway station near Kashmere Gate. I thought perhaps I would get a job somewhere nearby so I can get some money and I can somehow survive.' An old shopkeeper pitied me, Milkha recalls; he got a job at ₹10 per month. The shopkeeper would also bring him a roti and an onion from his own home. 'This is how my life started.'

Milkha tried to enlist during an army recruiting drive, but thousands applied for the handful of available posts. He applied at least twice more but was rejected each time.

By then, Milkha had moved into the camp at Old Fort. Even there, conditions were tough, with not enough tents for everyone. Soon after, he would learn that his sister had also made it to Delhi, and lived in Shahdara. He moved to join her. Milkha's life spiralled further downwards as he was arrested and put in jail for travelling without a ticket on the train.

With his brother's help, Milkha finally managed to enrol in the army. And this would be the turning point in his life. 'I always give the credit of my success to the army because the army knows how to make a person work hard, how to maintain discipline.'

The next decade and a half of Milkha's life is a story of determination and the power of the human spirit.

In an internal army track meet, Milkha's athletic talents were discovered. He was put on a special diet and training schedule. Initially, inspired only by the extra dietary supplements and milk, Milkha would soon find his feet, literally, as a great athlete.

He was selected for the Melbourne Olympics, but lost in the first round itself. 'When I came back from Melbourne, I promised myself that until I do not break the world record, I will not sit idle.' The athlete within Milkha was born. He remembers those years. 'I used to run for 6–7 hours in the strong summer heat. People used to say, "He will die", "This person is mad, he is mad". But Milkha's hunger for success was great.

'We have to resist our problems,' emphasizes Milkha. 'Only I know that I didn't have food to eat, didn't have clothes to wear, didn't have a house to live in, and didn't have water to drink, I had nothing. But how long will you keep sleeping hungry? If you won't move forward in life, then you will die of hunger. I feel if there is one lesson from my life it is that I suffered many problems, but I overcame each one of them. When you have a problem, God also gives you a solution.'

He trained relentlessly. 'Countless times I vomited blood, countless times blood came out of my urine, but I was determined that I wanted to break the world record,' he remembers. And he did break records. In 1957, he broke the national records in both the 400-metre and 200-metre races. The following year, he set a new Asian record. He won the Asian Games in Tokyo in both the races; and the 440 yards in the Commonwealth Games. This was followed by a string of victories around the world in the next few years in both

145

the 400-metre and 200-metre races, with Milkha winning 77 of his 80 international races, and breaking and setting his own world records repeatedly.

But along with the victories, there is one loss etched into his memory. 'I have only cried a few times in my life. Once was when the Partition happened and my parents were killed in front of my eyes; another was when I was at the Delhi Railway Station. The next time I cried was during the 1960 Rome Olympics—the Gold [medal] which I had to win for India, which I narrowly missed, and with which 15 years of my hardship were wasted.' Milkha puts it down to a split second's bad decision of slowing down at a crucial moment in the race.

As Milkha looks back on his life, he sees all the twists and turns. 'I went back to Pakistan in 1960. I didn't want to go. All of the things that happened with my parents, with my brother and sister, those scenes kept playing in front of my eyes, so I said I would not go for the sports meet in Pakistan. But Pandit Jawaharlal Nehru convinced me that I must go.'

'When I went back to our village, it felt very good. I cried a lot when I got there. I cried a lot when those scenes of my family's killing came into my mind. I found out that the friend who I used to go to school with had been orphaned during the Partition, but adopted by our Muslim teacher who raised him. He was married with kids. Some girls from our village who had been abducted and converted during that time were also still there. Though many had died, one or two were there, and they remembered me. I got a lot of respect when I was there in 1960. It made me realize that people are not bad, it is the politics that tears us apart.' It was here in Pakistan that he would get the name that would stick with him for the rest of his life—The Flying Sikh. After he defeated Abdul Khaliq in Lahore, General Ayub Khan gave him this moniker.

Today, Milkha tries to support those less fortunate than him. He has set up a charitable trust to support the children of impoverished sportspersons by taking care of their education, their healthcare and other needs. He also supports the children of fallen soldiers. It is a support borne of his own realization of the vagaries of fate.

Milkha emphasizes that his story is not one of overnight or easy success. 'After watching the film, *Bhaag Milkha Bhaag**, all of India wants to become Milkha Singh. All of them are coming up to me—doctors, engineers—all of them saying, "We want to become Milkha Singh". But becoming Milkha Singh is not an easy job, I did 15 years of hard work to achieve what I did.' Today, looking back, he notes, it is easy just to see the highlights and the successes, without realizing the daily determination and the sacrifices. 'Was Milkha Singh made in one day? I ran 80 races around the world. It was only because every month and every year my name was highlighted in newspapers, that I have achieved fame over 15 years. No one can make their name in one day, and most are deterred just by the first time they vomit blood, few are willing to undertake the hardships required for success.

'Without hardship, without discipline, without willpower, without hard work, no person can move forward, no person can be successful. I kept striving for 15 years. Be it day or night, Milkha Singh kept running.'

**Bhaag Milkha Bhaag* (which translates to 'Run Milkha Run') is a 2013 Hindi motion picture based on Milkha Singh's life that was directed by Rakeysh Omprakash Mehra.

A Refugee Fights for Other Refugees' Rights

Ram Jethmalani

Born: 14 September 1923 in Shikarpur, Bombay Presidency,
British India (now in Sindh, Pakistan)

*Ram Jethmalani is commonly known as India's highest paid lawyer.
He is a sitting member of the Rajya Sabha, and has previously
served as the Union Minister of Law and Justice and as Union
Minister of Urban Development.*

'I was born in a place called Shikarpur, in the Sindh province of pre-Partition India. I practised law in Karachi until it became impossible for us to stay there in safety, and we had to migrate to Bombay [now Mumbai]', begins Ram Jethmalani, the renowned 95-year old lawyer.

Ram was born on 14 September 1923 in an affluent Sindhi family. His father and grandfather were both lawyers.

Ram's mother was only 14 years old when he was born, so he remembers her as more of an elder sister. His first sibling was born when he was eight years old. By then, Ram was already in school, and performing exceedingly well. Within a mere three months of entering first standard, he received a double promotion to the third standard, and shortly thereafter, again to the fifth standard. He matriculated at age 13 and completed law school at age 17.

The rules at that time did not allow people under 21 years of age to practise, so this became Ram's first legal battle. 'I fought my own litigation at seventeen and a half. I had found out that when I joined the Law College, this rule did not exist. It came into existence after I had made my choice. So, I argued my own case before Sir Godfrey Davis, the Chief Justice of Sindh, that it could not be retroactively applied to me.' He won, gaining the right to start his practice at the young age of 18.

The same year, 1941, he had an arranged marriage to 16-year-old Durga Ahuja.

Ram's legal acumen was immediately apparent. Soon after entering law, he partnered with Allahbuksh Brohi to start a law firm, Brohi & Co. 'He was a qualified lawyer, but he was employed as a teacher. Due to his difficult economic circumstances, he felt that he could not give up a stable job and take to legal practice. I told my father that now you will have to look after one more son, so he helped us start an office together. I convinced Brohi to resign from his job and come with me as a Senior Partner in the firm.

'He was a philosopher really,' remembers Ram. 'He was extremely well-read on Buddha and Kant, he would attend lectures in the Theosophical Society in Karachi. I really admired him.'

While Brohi focussed on finding clients, Ram focussed on the cases. Their law firm started getting all the major legal cases in Karachi as Ram built a reputation as a formidable lawyer. He worked 16-hour days, poring over the law and formulating innovative arguments.

But within a few years, fate interrupted. The riots had started in many parts of India in 1946, spreading like wildfire to the Punjab region in 1947. 'There was a lot of communal tension outside Sindh. Though Sindh was still peaceful, the talk of Partition was in the air.'

Sindh had been separated from the Bombay Presidency in 1936 and was now a Muslim majority province. However, it was one that prided itself on a syncretic culture. People from the region viewed themselves as Sindhis first and Hindus or Muslims second, so there was no sense amongst the Hindus that they might have to leave. In fact, even after Partition became a reality in August 1947, most Sindhi Hindus believed they would stay on. Unlike Punjab, that saw a mass migration on religious lines from east to west, and west to east between August and December 1947, the large majority of Hindu Sindhis did not leave in 1947. It was only in 1948 that this exodus started in Sindh too.

As refugees from East Punjab crossed into Pakistan, many

came to Karachi, the then capital of Pakistan. This changed the dynamics in Sindh. These refugees had been displaced from their homes and brought with them tales of misery and violence. 'It wasn't the Muslim Sindhis—we shared a very lovely relationship with them. When Partition happened, Muslims from other regions arrived. It was these outsiders who created problems. But even they did not want to kill us, they only wanted our property. We loved Sindh, but it became increasingly impossible for us to live in Pakistan.'

As the uncertainty of the situation grew, and fear spread amongst the Sindhi population, some families chose to send their women, children and elderly members ahead. The men stayed back to guard the homes and businesses on the assumption that eventually their family would return. The same happened in Ram's family. He also had to stay back as his brother-in-law was unwell and could not move immediately.

'I sent my family across to Bombay by ship and stayed back in Sindh.'

His wife, along with their two daughters, moved into her parents' house in Bombay, and thus, avoided the squalor of camp life. But Ram's parents, his sisters and grandparents were not so fortunate. They were allotted a room in a refugee camp set up in abandoned army barracks near Pune. The family remembers the squat buildings with four families in a row, with just a hole in the ground for sanitary purposes. Ram was horrified to see these conditions when he arrived later, and a biographer notes that he vowed then never to be poor again.*

Ultimately, Ram too found that he had to leave Sindh. This

---

*From *The Rebel: A Biography of Ram Jethmalani* by Susan Adelman, published by Shobhaa De Books, 2014.

was in February 1948, after a major incident where a number of Sikhs taking refuge in a gurdwara in Karachi were burnt alive. Ram had been in office when the riots started, and he had to disguise himself to make his way back home safely; he hid there for three days, but finally realized that staying on further in Sindh at that time was impossible. Brohi too felt that he could no longer protect Ram. 'Things became too bad for anybody to stay.'

Ram left Karachi for Bombay on 18 February 1948.

Brohi offered to find a way to send him money. 'When I came to Bombay, he called me every week saying "Ram, all the money I earn is actually yours. Just tell me what you want and I will have it sent to you." But I used to tell him that "Brohi, I am testing my manhood here and I am trying myself. I don't want any money. But be sure that I know that you are available to me and some day if I am terribly in need, I will certainly make a demand on you."

'The only time that I used my friend Brohi was when I purchased the car and the owner of the car wanted the money in Pakistan because he was migrating from India. So, I remember that Brohi paid for that car.'

When Ram went to meet his family, he saw their squalid living conditions, and found that his father was in a deep depression because of all the changes Partition had wrought. Ram was only 25 at that time, but he had to take control of the family and their finances.

He started to look for ways to re-establish his law practice. He moved to Bombay with another Sindhi refugee, and they rented a room in a cheap guesthouse. His family stayed in a house in Ulhasnagar outside Bombay. He also rented an office for his father there and tried to encourage him out of his depression back into practice.

Fate was kind, and Ram managed to manoeuvre a property exchange with a Muslim who was leaving for Karachi. He followed up to attain an allotment order from the Bombay Land Requisition Authorities. This way they got a home in Bombay.

Ram was, at this time, still struggling to make ends meet. He had to support his grandparents, parents, sisters, wife and daughters; apart from his father's small practice, they all relied on his income.

He briefly considered taking a job as a magistrate for the income, but decided that his heart was in being a lawyer. He rented just enough space in an office for a table to meet clients, sharing the office with a cotton merchant.

Partition had made him a refugee. But in a twist of fate, it was the cases he fought for refugee rights that in turn re-established him.

153

The first such case was against a strict legislation called the Bombay Refugee Act, 1948. 'When I came to Bombay, I felt that we were not treated like guests in dismay and deserving sympathy and help, but as if we had come as some kind of unwanted people. They had passed The Bombay Refugees Act. It treated us like we were prisoners. They could shift us from one place to another, keep us where they liked and all kinds of things.' The law noted that the state could decide where refugees could reside and where they would be rehabilitated; the state had used it to evict Sindhis and to restrict their movement. Ram filed a Public Interest Litigation (PIL) against the Act on the grounds that it was unconstitutional, and he won.

Soon after, he fought another case regarding the Sindhi script. The Sindhi language had been traditionally written in a modified Arabic script with additional letters. However, the Bombay legislature noted that it should be written in the Devnagiri script (which Hindi and Sanksrit use). Ram filed another PIL, and in 1950, an order was passed that either script could be used in schools.

He was not even thirty years old at the time, but he already found himself positioned as the saviour of the Sindhi refugees. 'Within less than two years, I made my name,' he recalls.

Other refugee cases came forward. Some Sindhis had heard of him from Karachi, others approached him through these cases; so many of the refugees had legal problems— someone had a dispute over rent, someone else over obtaining or retaining their property, someone in a criminal case. Ram fought many cases in the small causes court in those days, but his practice slowly picked up, and the high-profile PIL cases had helped him get noticed by the elite lawyers also.

From then, there was almost no looking back. Ram got married a second time in 1952 and fashioned an unusual arrangement with his two wives and families. He began to save his earnings, and soon, he and his second wife Ratna joined the social scene in Bombay.

By the late 1950s, he had plenty of work. By the 1960s, they had purchased a nice, new apartment.

Ram's practice grew rapidly because of his pragmatic approach. He was willing to defend almost anyone. In those days of License Permit Raj, smuggling was at high levels, and Ram came to have a reputation as a 'Smuggler's Lawyer'. This pragmatism helped him fully re-establish the family wealth.

By 1957, less than 10 years after arrival, and at the age of 34, Ram argued his first case in the Supreme Court.

But he really shot to fame a few years later with the Nanavati case, which was widely covered by the tabloids.

Though he did not actually represent either side in this high-drama case of a naval officer who had shot his wife's lover, Ram supported the public prosecutor from the outside on behalf of the deceased man's sister (who was a Sindhi). His involvement was regularly reported on in news magazines like *Blitz* that gave daily updates on the case that had captured the imagination of the public. Soon, a second high-profile case, where a sadhu had seduced one of his followers, led to even more media coverage. The media loved this freewheeling lawyer who could be guaranteed to give some good quotes.

By the early 1960s, Ram had fully re-established the career he had lost at Partition. By 1970, he was appointed as the President of the Bar Council of India. In 1971, Ram entered politics and contested elections as an Independent with outside support from the Shiv Sena and Jana Sangh. He lost. However, in 1977, when he contested in Bombay, he won by a large margin.

The loss of his homeland stayed with Ram. Later in life, Ram headed a committee to try and find solutions to the Kashmir dispute. His friendships with decision-makers on both sides of the border positioned him well as an interlocutor.

Through all this time, he had not, however, lost touch with his mentor and friend, Brohi. In 1953, Brohi became Law Minister of Pakistan. A few years later, he became High Commissioner of Pakistan to India. 'I used to travel, in those days, from my home in Bombay to Delhi for my cases in the Supreme Court. Brohi would say, "I will not allow you to stay anywhere else," and so I would stay with him in his official residence on those trips to Delhi.'

Fate had separated two friends in 1947—one went on to

become the Law Minister of Pakistan in 1953, the other, some forty years later, the Law Minister of India in 1996. They never lost touch with each other till the former's death in 1987.

There Was No Compassion on Anyone's Face

Satish Gujral

Born: 25 December 1925 in Jhelum, undivided Punjab
(now in Pakistan)

Satish Gujral is one of the most eminent painters, sculptors and muralists in India today. He was awarded the Padma Vibhushan (1999) and was feted as Indian of the Year (2014) by NDTV. His paintings have received much critical and popular acclaim; one of the paintings of his Partition series recently sold for $1,25,000.

The agony seems to swirl off the canvas onto reality in Satish Gujral's Partition paintings. 'I witnessed killing, murder, rape,'* he says. 'I painted the cruelty of man.'

His father had been a staunch freedom fighter. So, when Partition happened, Gujral and his father stayed back in Pakistan to help refugees to safety in convoys. Those seven months of almost weekly trips between Jhelum and Jalandhar escorting refugee families, haunted Gujral for a long time and drove him to give voice to those memories through his art in the following year.

Gujral's introduction to art, however, had happened much earlier. He was born in Jhelum, now in Pakistan, in the winter of 1925. As a young boy, at the tender age of eight, Gujral suffered a terrible tragedy when an accident caused him to lose his hearing. He remembers the shock of the morning, when he woke up and was surprised to hear no chirping birds, no whirr of the water pump; it was only when he called out to his mother, and she came, and he saw her lips moving but could hear no sound, that her distraught realization would lead him also to realize that the silence that had descended on him was there to stay.

'My fear was not so much about my hearing, as of the silence around. Finally, by evening, after many other tests, it became clear, that silence has come to stay with me,' Gujral recounted in *Metamorphosis*, a film on his life.†

He slowly withdrew into himself. But his worried father, Avtar Narain was determined to ensure that his son still

Brush with Life, by Sujata Kulshreshtha, produced by Wide Angle Films and Public Diplomacy Division, Government of India, 2011.
†*Metamorphosis*, by Sujata Kulshreshtha, produced by Wide Angle Films, 2013.

flourished. He initially enrolled him in a new school for the deaf and mute, but soon pulled him out when he realized that in picking up sign language, Gujral was forgetting the spoken language he already knew. Back home, Gujral had a difficult time adjusting in a silent world. One day, Avtar Narain, seeing his son's doodles, was inspired to send him to Mayo School of Art in Lahore; initially, the school allowed Gujral to just sit in on classes without being a formal student, but within a year, recognizing his talent, they gave him official admission. His time in Mayo would be instrumental in giving him an ability to work across multiple mediums and forms, from painting to sculpture to architecture.

This childhood tragedy gave Gujral a new way to express himself. 'Deafness has played a great role in my life. When I lost sound, I searched for an alternative. Motion is a substitute, otherwise it is stillness; so, the first thing I wanted to paint was motion.'*

His time as an artist had started. He went to JJ School of Art in Mumbai. But a leg injury from childhood continued to give him trouble, so he returned to Lahore. Soon, he set up a graphic studio there.

But shortly thereafter, Partition broke. 'The time when the talks of Partition were ongoing, nobody believed that it would ever happen. Everyone thought they were just speculations and that the country could never be divided,' Gujral recalls.

Later, when the decision of Partition had been finalized, he was in Lahore. 'But nobody knew what will happen to Lahore. Whenever two Hindus and Muslims met, they only had one question—"Where do you think Lahore will go?" Many people

*Ibid.

There Was No Compassion on Anyone's Face

thought that Lahore would be given to India because many businesses and institutions belonged to the Hindus.'

'One day, when I looked outside, I saw hundreds of women, men, children carrying beds and suitcases on their heads and running. Behind them there was a mob.' It was early August. Soon after that, Nehru visited Lahore. 'I still remember graphically that someone was saying "It's Nehru! It's Nehru!" We saw Pandit ji get out of the car, and immediately say, "Take me to the refugee camp". But the crowd was turning violent with despair, so the police advised him to leave. Four of us, including my father and I, went with him to a meeting nearby. We entered a small room and sat around a table. Pandit ji was extremely quiet. I still remember that scene clearly. After a while, Pandit ji turned his face towards my father and said, "Lalaji, do you think there is hope that Hindus will stay in Pakistan?" My father said, "No". He (Pandit ji) said, "Now you have broken my heart," adding that, "In the morning, I flew from Delhi and when I looked down I saw kaafila after kaafila moving from both sides. But I thought that after reaching Lahore, I will get some hope, but it is the same here."'

Gujral remembers, how in that meeting, Nehru also confided in his father that Lahore would go to Pakistan. Avtar Narain had been deeply involved in the freedom struggle for a long time. He had worked closely with Lala Lajpat Rai, particularly supporting him in the agitations against the Simon Commission. He went to jail many times; as did his wife, and Gujral's other siblings. Soon after Partition, he took on the role of liaison officer for the Rawalpindi Division, helping evacuate refugees.

Gujral was 21 at that time. He decided to go with his father to Jhelum to help with the evacuation work. 'Normally, it takes about two and a half to three hours. But that day in the car, it took us the entire day because after every five steps murders and killings were taking place.

'There was a member of the Pakistani Assembly, Raja Ghazanfar Ali, who was a friend of my father. When he came to know that my father was heading towards Jhelum, he said that he would come along. All the way he said, "Lalaji, we should try our best in convincing Hindus to stay back here." My father sorrowfully looked at all the murders around him and he had no answer to give. When we reached Jhelum, a mob had also reached there. They surrounded our house. It was only Raja's intervention—he spent an entire day convincing the mob to leave—that was the only way we all managed to stay alive. Otherwise, that night none us would have survived.'

Gujral and his father spent the next seven months evacuating refugees. 'Once every week, we used to go to Amritsar or Jalandhar with a convoy from Jhelum. We used to drop off some refugees and then go back.

'Once we were going back from Jalandhar to Jhelum, and on the way, we saw that there was a big mob assembled and the car couldn't move forward. I got off and went forward to see what was happening and I saw that the mob had surrounded a girl. They were taking the girls, undressing them in the square, and were raping and murdering them. The people just stood watching. I've described the scene in these words in my writing: "I looked in all four directions to see if there was compassion on anyone's face. But I saw that there was absolutely no compassion. After all these years, when I sit and wonder about was the biggest loss incurred during the Partition? Money, property, home, life? No. It was the loss of compassion. I looked around and there was no compassion on anyone's face.'" Gujral recalls sadly, 'This is just one in many instances. I used to travel every week...'

Another time: 'Once, on the edge of Chenab river, at night, there was a heavy tide and all the men, women, children, animals in the kaafilas that had stopped there, got swept away. The next day, when we passed by there, there was this unbearable odour, and we realized how many people had died.'

Gujral and his family also worked to rehabilitate and rescue abducted women. He recalls one incident where a girl got left behind. 'She didn't know what to do. The house next to hers belonged to a Muslim landlord who was a good friend of her father, so she went to his house. He gave her refuge and told her that he would protect her. But when the mob got to know, they threatened that they would kill her. The landlord realized that the only way to protect her was to marry her. Meanwhile, we got to know that this girl is trapped in this village and decided to rescue her. But we were deeply troubled about how to do it, because most people from this village were retired Army men and they were all armed. I remember the scene. It was late night and very dark, we arrived there by car. We managed to rescue the girl and bring her to Jhelum, some 40 miles away. My father was worried that this news would spread, so he told me to take her immediately to India. The following day when the landlord came to know what had happened, he came to Jhelum. At first, he kept insisting that he had come to take the girl back, and my father kept insisting that she wasn't there. But after a while, the landlord started weeping and said to my father, "You have saved me from a big decision. I didn't want to keep her that way but it was the only way..." We had been worried he had come to murder us, but just like that he went away.'

Gujral remembers that over the course of those seven months, they rescued nearly a hundred women. 'Every time we went, we were scared if we would even make it back.' His mother meanwhile helped to set up an ashram at Jalandhar for these girls. 'When we started to rescue women, I initially dropped them at home with my mother in Jalandhar. But when the numbers grew, my mother realized that a more permanent solution was needed, so she started a Nari Ashram.'

It was ultimately only when they stopped getting any further news of women hiding or in need of rescue, that the father and son felt they could go to India and join their family. 'When a month had gone by and there was no news of any woman or girl who was hiding, we thought that we'd completed our work.'

When they left, they were themselves able to bring very little with them. 'We gave our neighbour the key to our house, and left. Never again did I go back to Jhelum. My heart wanted to. I went to Lahore twice. Not Jhelum. It's strange, every time I went to Lahore, I fell ill and couldn't go further.' Years later, on one such trip, lying in the hospital bed in Lahore, Gujral looked out of the window and recognized the jail that his mother had once been imprisoned in during the freedom struggle.

After Partition, the family tried to build their life anew in India. Gujral's father became a judge, and his brother came to Delhi to join politics. Gujral returned to his art.

'When I started to paint, it never crossed my mind that I was painting Partition, but what came out was Partition. If an artist thinks first and paints later, there will be no truth.' Gujral's paintings reflected the anguish of what he had seen in those seven months.

'Six months after Partition, I painted the cruelty of man.'

There Was No Compassion on Anyone's Face

He picked subjects around him to reflect the grief. A painting of a young boy in sorrow was based on the gardener's son; a painting of women in mourning was based on his mother and sister. All the suffering, the anguish came out in his paintings. 'Many years passed and only slowly that grief gave away, and I painted differently because the pain had passed,' reflects Gujral. But in those early years the anguish swirled on his canvas; perhaps accentuated by the continuing silence that enveloped his life.

Gujral soon got a job as an artist in the Punjab government, and fate opened the doors wide shortly after.

His Partition series received a lot of critical acclaim. In 1952, he received a fellowship to go to Mexico and work with the famed muralist Diego Rivera.

For someone who still lived in a world of silence, and barely spoke any English, the fear of what lay ahead daunted him on his boat journey. 'The first three months were terrible because of the language difficulty, but still I could go around the museums and see the murals of Rivera, Oruzco and others.'* He pushed himself to pick up enough Spanish and English to communicate.

In Mexico, Gujral apprenticed with Rivera and Sequieros, and became close friends with Frida Kahlo. This period had an enormous influence on his work.

When he returned to India in 1955, the art scene in India was slowly opening up. Though individual buyers were few, some corporates were looking for murals and art to decorate their offices. Artists, groups had sprung up. Gujral moved in with his brother, Inder (who later became the twelfth Prime

---

*Ibid.

Minister of India).

With Inder's help, Gujral got commissioned to do a series of political images that helped establish him. The first of these was a portrait of Lala Lajpat Rai, his father's political mentor. This went on to adorn the Central Hall of Parliament. Soon, he would make one of Nehru. 'I used to go to Teen Murti House every four days to paint him. My brother also accompanied me to interpret. One day, my brother told Nehru that I had been in Nehru's life twice. Nehru asked, "Twice? When was the first time?" I repeated the story of that day in Lahore in August 1947.'

It was around this time that Gujral met the one person who would radically change his life—his future wife Kiran. She too had moved at the time of Partition; her father had been a leading dentist in Lahore. Now she was studying art in Delhi. The courtship was rapid and intense. But they faced resistance from Kiran's parents who did not approve of their daughter marrying a penniless artist, who then still had not established himself.

Those early years were hard financially for Satish and Kiran Gujral. Often, they did not have money for rent or bus fares, but Gujral was determined to make art his vocation. Kiran stood by him, and became his bridge to the rest of the world. She interpreted for him and reduced the void of silence around him. Slowly his paintings began to reflect the exuberance and joy of this partnership.

In the 1960s, with the government's push on industrialization under Pandit Nehru, new buildings started coming up across Delhi, and Gujral was commissioned to contribute to many of these with large murals and works.

But just as he would become comfortable and start to

establish himself in one style, Gujral would change direction; this happened numerous times in his career. He constantly chose his artistic vision and growth over the monetary comfort of a single path. At this stage, he turned to making paper collages; these were little understood or appreciated in the Indian art market of that time, though they got some interest abroad. After this he moved to using industrial waste and mirrors to make sculptures and then, to a burnt wood sculpture series.

Because he was often ahead of his time, his works would not gain immediate acceptance, and Kiran and he struggled monetarily. But still Gujral followed his inner voice, always trying to push himself out his comfort zone.

In 1984, Gujral pushed the boundaries even further when he moved into architecture, much to the disdain of many at that time who viewed art and architecture as two very distinct fields. However, Gujral had a vision. He applied for, and won, an international competition to design the Embassy of Belgium in New Delhi. This got him much critical acclaim, including a high honour from the Belgian government—the Order of the Crown. He also went on to design many more high-profile buildings like the summer palace of the Shah of Iran in Dubai, and the Ambedkar Memorial Park in Lucknow.

In 1998, at age of 73, Gujral got a cochlear implant enabling him to hear for the first time in over six decades. After 64 years, he heard the sound of his own voice, and for the first time he heard Kiran's. 'I addressed Kiran and I asked her how she felt about my coming out of deafness and she said, "...For me, you have never been deaf."'[*]

*Ibid.

But after the initial exuberance of hearing again, Gujral realized that the sounds were too muffled for him to separate, too confusing. He found himself unable to paint. 'I asked myself what I wanted—painting or hearing? And I chose painting.'* Gujral embraced his world of silence once again.

His zest for finding new forms and arenas continues to grow even in his nineties.

But even though Gujral moved through many themes and forms in his life, the Partition stayed with him. He continues to support the ashram started in 1947 for the rehabilitation of the abducted women who were rescued.

---

*Ibid.

A Natural Disaster, and a Man-made Catastrophe

Swinder Singh Gandhi

Born: August 1929 in Quetta, Balochistan
(now in Pakistan)

Swinder Singh Gandhi could not complete his education due to his father's death in 1946, followed by Partition in 1947. However, that did not stop him from becoming the CEO of leading organizations, like McDowell & Company. He retired as the CEO of a major brewing company in South Africa.

Although he belonged to a relatively well-to-do family of Quetta in Balochistan, Swinder Singh Gandhi's life would take many twists and turns even before Partition.

The first mishap came in 1935 when the Quetta earthquake happened. 'It was one of the biggest disasters of the twentieth century—in the few minutes of the earthquake, some 30,000 people died,' recalls Swinder.

His own family too was deeply impacted. 'We also lost five members of the family—my grandfather, my grandmother, one uncle and two brothers. I was just about six years old at that time, but I vividly recall watching my father cremate the five bodies together.' It was deeply traumatic.

The family had to move into a camp for some time. 'My first experience of the refugee camps was in 1935,' recalls Swinder. 'Though we had earlier seen the atrocities perpetrated by the British army, here in the aftermath, we also saw the British help with the relief work. All the communities—Hindus, Muslims, Sikhs—also helped each other and lived in the camps together.'

The earthquake, which had been 7.7 on the Richter scale, also devastated their trading business. 'My father had a business in distribution of foodgrains and consumer products—it was badly hit by the earthquake. I saw him struggling to rebuild his business after the earthquake,' remembers Gandhi.

Just as the family was beginning to find their feet again, another tragedy struck. Swinder's father passed away from cancer in 1946.

The young boy of 17, who had completed his matriculation the previous year, felt directionless. His elder brother was in Lahore and had just completed his MBBS degree and did not want to return to Quetta to run the business. 'With the death of my father, the business fell on my shoulders at a very young age. My educational career ended there.'

Swinder closely followed the politics of the time. 'At that time, the political situation in the country was in turmoil. The movement for the creation of Pakistan was gaining momentum. We heard on the radio about riots that had started from August 1946 in Calcutta, and in March 1947 in Punjab, but in Quetta it was completely peaceful. There were no riots at that time.

'There was a complete absence of any ill feeling between the two communities; this led us to think that we could stay there. In August 1947, right before Partition, Jinnah also spoke about how everyone would be treated equally so this encouraged us even more that we would not need to leave Quetta.'

'It was only later that things started getting bad. Outsiders arrived in Quetta, and then the slogans started—*Nara-e-Takbeer* and *Allah hu Akbar*.'

'One day, one of our Muslim friends told us that we should move out of our house because it was vulnerable to attack, so we moved into the Gurdwara for safety. Thankfully, we were already there when the mobs reached our house. My younger sister had fractured her leg and we were all very worried. My brother somehow managed to get two seats in a plane leaving Quetta, and he told me to take her to India.' The other members of the family were still left behind. 'My brother, my mother, my three sisters, along with my uncle's family—another three daughters and my aunt—were still there.'

Swinder was extremely anxious for their safety. Every day, through fellow refugees, through the radio, through the newspapers, he heard of the trains full of dead bodies moving in either direction, of the mutilation of victims' bodies, of rape and death. Fortunately, a Sikh regiment posted in Quetta evacuated the rest of the family in October.

With the family reunited, they had to decide how to rebuild their lives. 'When we arrived in India, we had very few resources because all our resources were deployed in the business in Quetta or in properties which we could not move. Very little cash was available with us.'

Swinder's brother managed to get a job as a doctor with the government in Uttar Pradesh, so the family moved to Agra, and somehow made ends meet for the extended family on his income.

Swinder started looking around for ways that he could contribute to their family income. 'To start a business you need capital, but I had none,' he remembers.

Because his brother was at the Medical College in Agra, Swinder started to get acquainted with doctors in the city. He realized that he could start a distribution business in disposal goods for doctors. 'I started purchasing disposal goods that belonged to the army and selling them to doctors. That is how I started my life... I had no one to guide me in the business world since my brother had never done business. But thankfully, I had a bit of experience from Quetta.

'I started travelling to Lucknow, Benaras, Allahabad on one side, and Amritsar, Jalandhar on the other to sell these surgical instruments. It was just a one-man company at that time: Me. I did not have enough money to travel and stay in hotels so I would just sleep on the railway station platform or in the waiting rooms at stations.

'Those were difficult moments...but I got through them.'

For five years, the young man struggled. 'In 1952—as they say, God opens doors for you—there was a surgeons' conference at the Agra Medical College. A lot of foreign companies brought their medical instruments there. There was a German company with one man who needed help to manage his stall at the exhibition centre. A professor in the Medical College Agra had told this gentleman to contact me to see if I would be interested in helping him. While I was managing the stall during the exhibition, a British company, Allen and Hanburys, who had the next stall, saw my work and appreciated it. Around nine months after this conference, they offered me a job. I accepted and I started my life at ₹350 per month. It was 5 July 1953 to be precise.'

Swinder performed well in the role. Though he had not completed his high school, much less an undergraduate or a postgraduate degree, his dedication and capabilities pushed him forward.

'One day, the managing director offered me the position of the Head of Department of Surgical Divisions. I was taken aback because there were so many people who were more educated than me.'

This would be just the first step in a long, successful career built on his hard work. His next career transition would be to a company called Herbertsons in their chemicals division. There, Swinder would meet the man who would change the course of the rest of his life and career—Vithal Mallya.

When Swinder started working for Mallya, an immediate relationship of trust developed. 'Vithal Mallya was very clever; I would even say, he was a genius. He spoke very few words and in those few words you had to grasp what he was looking for. And if you could deliver, then you were his favourite. Fortunately, for me, some very critical projects under my charge got approved by the government, so I kept being given more and more responsibilities.'

After Vithal Mallya's death in 1983, his son, Vijay Mallya,

took the reins. Swinder was then 55 years old. In 1986, at age 58, Swinder retired. One day, in 1989, he got a call from Vijay Mallya's office: 'He told me, Swinder, during my father's time, you made us the market leader. The people who have succeeded you have not been able to sustain our market position as number one. I want you to come back and help me to restore the company to that status,' recalls Swinder, who then returned to the group as CEO of McDowell's Limited.

In 1996, a decade later, at age 67, Swinder retired for the second time.

But barely six months later, Mallya once again called him back to lead an exciting new growth venture in South Africa. A twelfth-class dropout, Swinder was now overseeing hundreds of MBAs from the world's most advanced universities in a multinational company that employed a few thousand people.

Finally, in 2002, he retired for the third time.

Meanwhile, as the family's financial condition improved, Swinder ensured that his two sons received the education that he himself had not been able to complete. One went on to do an MBA at Harvard Business School (and later teach there), the other at Wharton Business School. Fate had resulted in Swinder dropping out in the twelfth class, but it could not clip the wings of this meticulous and determined achiever.

We Flew the Pakistani Flag, Celebrated the End of British Rule, Still Had to Flee

Ved Marwah

Born: 15 September 1932 in Peshawar, North-West Frontier Province (now Khyber Pakhtunkhwa in Pakistan)

Ved Marwah served as the Governor of Manipur (1999–2003), Mizoram (2000–2001) and Jharkhand (2003–2004). He spent his career in the Indian Police Service, rising to become the Commissioner of Police, Delhi, and later the Director General of the National Security Guard (NSG). He was awarded the Padma Shri for his work in 1989.

'The June announcement of Partition came as a total surprise to us; till then, we had never believed that Partition would actually happen. But even after the June declaration, we believed that Partition would be quite peaceful, and that we could continue to live in Peshawar. On 14 August, we flew the Pakistani flag and declared ourselves as loyal Pakistani citizens and celebrated the end of the British rule. We didn't think that Partition, or living in Pakistan, would bring any change in our lives. The communal trouble in Peshawar started much later. We didn't leave till mid-November,' recalls Ved Marwah.

Ved was born in Peshawar on 15 September 1932, in a family that was comfortably well-off. His father, Faqir Chand Marwah, ran the Oriental Book Shop in Peshawar. Ved had two brothers and four sisters. He remembers his childhood town as one with a syncretic culture. 'Before Partition, there was absolutely no tension at all between communities; some of our neighbours were Muslims, our gardener was a Muslim, there was no problem at all. In school, Urdu was the first language,' he recalls. 'I still know how to read and write it perfectly. English was taught only after primary school. At home, we spoke Punjabi.

'But suddenly, things turned violent; we are just lucky that we survived.' In early September, a mob went on a rampage attacking Hindu and Sikh houses across the city. Ved recalls standing on a rooftop watching houses around them engulfed in smoke and flames. The family managed to successfully fend off an attack on their house but watched paralysed as their friends' and neighbours' houses were burnt down. Many came to find refuge in their home.

But Ved's father, Faqir Chand, was still determined not to

leave. He and his brothers had built their business in Peshawar and couldn't imagine leaving everything behind. It was only when the Deputy Commissioner, a friend and classmate of Faqir Chand, told him that he could no longer protect him, that Faqir Chand realized that the family would have to leave. The family had already been living in a state of siege for months, rarely venturing out; their shop had also been declared evacuee property, even though they had not left Peshawar.

'The Deputy Commissioner arranged a chartered flight for a few of us from Peshawar to Delhi, so we escaped the terrible train journey and violence. I remember that the seats were removed so that more people could fit inside. Our Muslim friends helped us get to the airport safely.

'My uncle didn't leave till February 1948. He hoped that things would calm down. Though his family had shifted, he stayed on hoping that we will all come back. But eventually the situation forced him to leave too.'

When the family arrived in Delhi, they had no place to stay. 'We had a very rough time in the beginning. We first went to the Hindu Mahasabha Bhawan; we were penniless and we had to sleep on the floor. But still we had a very peaceful sleep because at least there was no fear of attack. But we had nothing with us, absolutely nothing. We were lucky to escape with the clothes on.' Ved remembers the next few months as a traumatic restart, spending a few days here, a few days there, as they tried to find their feet in a new city. His education had also been completely disrupted; he wouldn't enrol again in school for over a year.

'We built our life again brick by brick. I did a clerk's job in the beginning for ₹100 a month and then began a stall in Regal Building from there. We kept shifting from place to place till we came to Khan Market. For some time in the army cantonment with a relative, then in Paharganj in Multani Dhanda. One of the flats we stayed at had been vacated by Muslims that had been pushed out. It was a very unfortunate time. One of the flats we stayed at in Rajinder Nagar was without water or electricity.'

In 1950, Ved enrolled in St. Stephen's College in Delhi for his BA in Economics, and later stayed on there to complete his Masters in History.

In 1951, Khan Market was established to rehabilitate Partition refugees, particularly traders from the NWFP. It was named after NWFP leader Khan Abdul Ghaffar Khan's elder brother, Khan Abdul Jabbar Khan. Shops were built on the ground floor, with residential flats on the first floor. In all, 154 shops and 74 flats were allocated.

Faqir Chand Marwah was allocated a shop and a flat and decided to restart the book business that he had left behind during Partition. He named the shop after himself: Faqir Chand and Sons. 'We got help from the government—that's how we survived. First, they gave us a loan of ₹3,000 to start our little business, and then much later, against the claims, we got a shop in Khan Market.'

Ved remembers a smaller, quieter Delhi of those days. 'Delhi was not such a noisy place. I was studying and working at the same time, so I would go sit in Connaught Place or Jantar Mantar, which were such nice, calm places then, and I would sit on a bench outside and study. Very different from today.' Khan Market too was of course not what it is today. Before 1947, Khan Market had had only a few small provision stores. Today, it is the most expensive real estate in India, and one of the most expensive in all of Asia, but for a long time it was a quiet neighbourhood market. 'Now, of course, Khan Market is prime property, but that time there were no shops; we were one of the first shops to open, there were very few customers.'

Though he had been helping at the shop throughout his university studies, after graduation, Ved decided to take a job with Caltex, and then soon after that, to take the exam for the services. He joined the Delhi Police in the batch of 1956 as Superintendent of Police, North District, and rose through the ranks over the decades to become Commissioner of Delhi Police from 1985 to 1988 and then the Director General, National Security Guard (NSG), from 1988 to 1990. During his long career, he also served as Joint Secretary, National Police Commission; First Secretary, High Commission of India, London; and Deputy Commissioner of Police, Calcutta.

For his exemplary service, Ved was awarded a Gallantry Medal from the Police, and the Padma Shri. After retirement from the police, Ved served as Governor of Manipur, Mizoram, and Jharkhand between the years 1999 to 2004.

Today, most of the refugee families have moved out of Khan Market. The shops have changed hands many times over. An article in 2015 in *The Times of India* estimated that ten or fewer of the flats are still occupied by families out of the 74 original flats; a branch of the Marwah family is one of the remaining residents. Faqir Chand and Sons is also still open, a testament to those early days of Khan Market. Anand Stationers and the Bahrisons bookshop are a few of the other original businesses. Faqir Chand and Sons bookshop is run today by some of the grandchildren and great grandchildren of Faqir Chand Marwah.

Post his retirement from the police force, Ved became

involved in Track II Diplomacy efforts between India and Pakistan. 'I was in Islamabad, and I told our hosts that I want to go to Peshawar, so they gave me a car, I drove down.

'I decided to find an old friend who used to live opposite the General Post Office. They had a carpet shop there. I found the shop and said, "I want to meet Samat Khan." The people there just stared at me for a while, then asked, "Where have you come from?" I replied, "From New Delhi." They told me that Samat Khan died quite a few years back. They insisted that they wanted to gift me a carpet as I was their guest. I didn't take it, but I was so touched that they genuinely wanted to present one to me.

'I wanted to see my old house. Unfortunately, when I reached there, I saw it was under demolition. I got a little emotional. The labour there came up to me and tried to console me. All they could say was, '*Tera makaan bahut pakka tha*' (Your house was very strong).

Acknowledgments

This book has been the culmination of the joint efforts of a number of people.

I must first thank and acknowledge the Partition Museum and The Arts and Cultural Heritage Trust. The saying goes 'it takes a village...', and in the case of this book that is entirely accurate. The oral histories profiled in this book are part of the collections of the recently opened Partition Museum at Town Hall, Amritsar. I must, therefore, thank the Trustees, Advisors, donors and supporters of the Museum, including particularly the Government of Punjab. I must also thank the team of the Partition Museum, and, in particular, Ganeev Kaur Dhillon and Tara Sami Dutt for their help in conducting many of the interviews that underlie this book, and overall for their passion and dedication to our common mission. I would also like to acknowledge the contribution of the following volunteers and interns who have helped in conducting or transcribing these interviews—Akshat Saxena, Ananya Narain, Charanjeet Singh, Deepanjali Chadha, Devina Dhimri, Janani Sekhar, Mansi Rawat, Mohammed Shahrukh, Nityah Wahi, Rishika Sharma, Saudiptendu Ray, Sneharshi Gupta, Steni Thomas, Supriti David, Ulfat Rana, Vishakha Khandelwal, Vishrut and Vridhi Tuli. Abhishek Rana helped with the photographs.

I would like to particularly acknowledge Kishwar Desai for a number of reasons. Firstly, the concept of this book truly belongs to her. As the visionary and driving force behind the establishment of the Partition Museum, she envisaged that the last gallery in the Museum, aptly named the Gallery of Hope, would pay a tribute to the resilience of all those millions who rose from the devastation of Partition to rebuild their lives and our nation. This is the same spirit in which this book is written, and the credit for the idea of the book belongs to her. Secondly, I must thank her for reviewing and providing comments on a draft of this book, as well as, ideating with me on its structure. She also conducted three of the interviews in this book.

I must of course also thank all the people profiled in this book who shared their stories with us so openly, as well as, all the people who helped us reach out to them. Last but not least, I must thank (and apologise to) Shambhu Sahu, Senior Commissioning Editor at Rupa Publications, who surely deserves some kind of award for patience for all the deadlines I let slip.